DEATH SMELLS OF CORDITE

Big Russ Farran is a millionaire who owns the Farran industrial empire. But he isn't so big when he finds an ex-G-man lying with a neat hole in his head. Now he's wanted by the cops and the FBI and, accused of murder, Farran's millions are no help to him. He must save himself. But first he must solve the mystery of who his enemy is — that ruthless, scheming mastermind who's framed him, and who wants his millions . . .

GORDON LANDSBOROUGH

DEATH SMELLS OF CORDITE

Complete and Unabridged

LINFORD
Leicester

First published in Great Britain

First Linford Edition
published 2010

Copyright © 1951 by Gordon Landsborough

British Library CIP Data

Landsborough, Gordon.
  Death smells of cordite.- -
  (Linford mystery library)
  1. Millionaires- -Crimes against- -Fiction.
  2. Suspense fiction.
  3. Large type books.
  I. Title II. Series
  823.9'14–dc22

  ISBN 978–1–84782–980–1

Published by
F. A. Thorpe (Publishing)
Anstey, Leicestershire

Set by Words & Graphics Ltd.
Anstey, Leicestershire
Printed and bound in Great Britain by
T. J. International Ltd., Padstow, Cornwall

1

Farran abruptly left his office and went across to the airframe shop. There was nobody there. There wouldn't be, of course. Only the backroom boys of the drawing office, the foremen and senior executives would be about the place — and they'd be sitting around reading or playing quiet crap, he guessed.

He climbed the gantry moodily, and looked across that enormous shop — the second biggest in the world, he had been told. Ford had the biggest at Red Willow.

There wasn't a stir of life, where usually it was busier than the Boulevard at Los Angeles, noisier with riveters than a ball game at the Bowl.

He looked down at the long line of aircraft — the nearest to him recognisable for what it was to be, almost completed; the farthest a mere skeleton of main spars and unclothed ribs. The biggest aircraft of their kind in the world — and a year behind schedule.

He stood there, high up in the streaming Californian sunshine, his lean figure throwing a two hundred foot shadow like an exclamation mark over the silent, unfinished work. And that quick, snapping anger filled him.

'Hell,' he thought, 'they'll be obsolete before they fly!'

They'd been so far ahead of competitors with their design, but these labour disputes had pulled them back until now they were probably no more advanced than some of the things other manufacturers were putting up . . .

And then a tiny thought seemed to lift in his mind. It was there for a fraction of a second, to be lost when something distracted him.

But it came — it was the first time there, and there must always be a first time. It dissolved in the contours of his memory cells, forgotten almost as soon as it came, but it would come again and perhaps next time it would be remembered . . .

That dark patch under the gigantic

wing of the first airframe was what distracted him. Blood. Left after the brawl of a few days ago, when some men hadn't wanted to strike.

He went down, went the way the boys went who couldn't be bothered to use the steps — crooked his feet around the handrails and slid down like an old-time fireman on his brass pole.

And it wasn't blood. It was oil stain. Someone must have cleaned up the traces of the brawl.

He stood under that fuselage, which towered twenty feet above him and would be still higher from the ground when the six-wheeled undercarriage was mounted.

It was all wing, almost. Swept back, and with turbo-jet engines mounted as pushers on the trailing edge — eight of them. And British, of course. The British were still ahead with aero-engines.

No room in the fuselage. Comparatively, that was. Space for the crew up forward, of course, and they could take a couple of jeeps or a few small field guns. That wasn't considered a load at all for aircraft as big as this.

And it was big — those wings were the biggest things that ever cast a shadow over earth, even though that earth had been concreted over in the airframe assembly shop. That was, excluding nature's clouds, of course.

They ought to be. Two hundred men would sit inside, one hundred in the port wing, one hundred to starboard. They'd sit and look ahead without any interruption to their vision; for the leading edge was almost continuous perspex.

Farran mooched out of the deserted shop thinking, 'I wouldn't like to sit up there. Not in real operations.' Yet he had flown Mustangs over France and Germany in that big beat-up at the time of the Second Front, and that hadn't worried him. But this was different, sitting with a hundred and ninety-nine other men, waiting to be dropped. Marines, they'd be, America's elite fighters. For these were the first of fifty troop carriers ordered by the U.S. Navy.

He went through the Administrative Block. There were a few people here, because work could go on for a time even without their ten thousand union-bound employees in the shops.

They jumped into frenzied action when they saw the boss walking the corridors, though the girls took care to let him see their nylons and flashed him their best, dressing table rehearsed smiles. A man who owned a multi-million dollar concern — and a few other odd investments — was quite a guy and worth a bit of hopeful bait. And when he was young with it, tough with it, and reasonably good-looking, well, a girl could even forget that flaming bad temper of his.

Just now he was moody. He didn't see them. He didn't know what to do, didn't know where to go. His life stopped when the pulse died in this gigantic aircraft works that his father had started as an offshoot to his aluminium alloy concern, now, comparatively, only another odd investment.

He paused outside the door marked *Labour Relations*. Uncle El would be there. El Farran who had talked with union leaders so long he looked like one. Heavy-jowled, leather-faced, as yellow as a time sheet. Be-glassed, with thick lenses so you couldn't quite see what was going on in his mind through betraying eyes.

Farran went into the department, putting everyone in a flurry, crossed to Uncle El's room and opened the door. The boss doesn't knock. Leastways, Russ Farran didn't.

Uncle El was on the phone. He was shouting for Washington. That was where the biggest crooks were, thought Farran cynically. Uncle El was swinging round in his swivel chair, jacket off, tie loosened. And bawling. Mad.

'What the — Washington, Washington . . . Yeah, yeah, that's the number I want . . . The hell, not there? Then why didn't you say so?'

Smash went the receiver on the stand, and Uncle El came whirling round. He liked to give an impression of a big shot tycoon, thought Farran cynically. He liked to be a man of power. Well, he was big enough; maybe too big, he thought. His father always swore he was the best Labour Relations Officer in the United States, and one time he'd seemed to be.

But not this last year. The Farran plant had the worst record for labour disputes anywhere.

Farran didn't understand it, couldn't. And that was why that triggering little thought that had come to him was important. Because he was beginning to think their record was too bad.

Uncle El saw him, stopped swinging. Farran couldn't see those eyes behind the lenses, but the glass itself gave an appearance of pale, dead-fish orbs.

El said, 'That was Washington.'

Farran said, 'It sounded like Washington.' Whenever you had dealings with Washington you got good and mad.

Then Uncle El just sat and said nothing more. Farran couldn't think of anything to say, so after a few seconds he nodded and went back into the corridor. Then he decided to go down to the gate and see the pickets.

As he came up to where the gate police were, just inside the high, steel-meshed gates, the public address system began its daily dose to the strikers.

Uncle El had had those loudspeakers

fixed up on the edge of the car park after the first strike nearly a year ago. He was a pretty smart man, Uncle El; he made sure that he could get a hearing with the strikers with those powerful broadcast units.

Farran couldn't tell what he was saying. You never could when you were on this side of the fence, because the loudspeakers were directed out towards the car park where the strikers were.

The announcement stopped as he went through the gate. There was the 'wedge' at the gate, that group of sullen, tough faced pickets whose duty it was to make a solid barrier across the gateway when would-be workers or trucks tried to go in. Not that anyone had entertained such thoughts for a few days now.

The main body of pickets had made themselves comfortable on the edge of the car park. They had plenty of room. There weren't two hundred cars where normally two thousand workers' vehicles stood.

The strike leader had got a caravan parked, so that he was always on the spot for talks. The boys had fixed him with electric light and a telephone, so that he could ring his wife and tell her how he much he missed her, the liar. For themselves they'd got beach chairs on the concrete, and there was more card-playing and dice-throwing than you'd see even downtown on a Sunday.

When Farran came out the card-playing stopped. Every eye came round to the boss. He gave them the eye back, and some shuffled and looked quickly away. While he was watching a truck trundled to a stop and opened up. It was the chuck wagon for the picket. Some of the strikers went up to it immediately, but most stood and watched what Farran was going to do.

He went over to look at the wagon. It was a properly equipped mobile food bar, all streamlined and chromium.

Farran said, 'You sure do yourselves well.'

The smell of hot coffee came richly to his nose, and there were hotdogs and hamburgers in the hot box to make the afternoon even more aromatic.

A big man, first in the queue, came round with a mouthful of hamburger and sneered, 'Why not, brother? Guess you don't do bad yourself with all your millions.'

Farran had seen him before at the gate. He was always there, the most assiduous striker. And the toughest. He came back with his mouth at the slightest opportunity. His raucous, irritating voice prompted Farran to mentally dub him the 'yawp'. That's what he was.

Farran looked at him. He was nearly his own height, but heavier. Much heavier. There was a pile of stomach trying to bust the strap he wore around his pants. And the pants looked sleep-weary, as if he bedded down in them. The face wasn't as soft-looking as the middle, though it was stubbly-unshaven and the hair looked as though it had been scratched on rising and not otherwise combed since. A tough, mocking face.

Farran said, 'I won't have many millions left, soon. This strike's costing me half a million a week. You figure how long I can last before it'll be no good picketing the place any more.'

But it didn't shake the strikers any. They knew modern finance and economics now. Knew that the Farran plant couldn't die, couldn't go out of existence, no matter how much it lost. They wouldn't scrap the Boulder Dam even though it was losing millions a year. Or the whole of the Tennessee Valley scheme. Or Fords or Boeings or Lockheeds, to bring it nearer to aviation.

Because they were national assets. With war apparently never far ahead such firms couldn't be allowed to die.

Anyway, in the fat years the Treasury took most of their profits, and when they had a lean year, as this, they were able to draw back. So it didn't matter a damn, in many ways, and the wise guys knew it.

The yawp said, brusquely, 'It don't cost you nothin'. But it costs the workers more'n half a million bucks a week in lost pay. I don't give no tears for the poor li'l rich fellar called Farran no more.'

Farran heard an admiring, 'Just lissen to Mac! He ain't scared of no one!'

'Scared?' Sag-belly scratched under his

shirt. 'What in hell's there anything to be scared of in this fellar?'

It got Farran mad. 'By God,' he snarled, 'some day you'll be back at your job. So help me, when that day comes I'll be after your hide, fellar!'

'You got me scared,' said the big yawp, but his sneer was twice as big. 'You want another strike when this one's over? You want another walkout because I'm bein' victimised, huh?'

Shooting off his mouth he was, standing up to the boss and being truculent. And the other men watched and admired. It was as well that someone stood up to Russ Farran, they thought; few men ever did.

The big yawp finished and shouted up another coffee and hamburger. Farran complained, 'I don't suppose the boss gets more'n a smell of that coffee?'

The yawp spoke with a mouth full. 'Brother, you supposed right. This is for the oppressed workers.'

'Oppressed? God knows what you're striking for now!'

And he didn't. They'd been in and out

so often, especially in the last six months, he couldn't quite remember what it was this time. Something to do with the social security scheme.

He left the pickets in full enjoyment of better hamburgers than he'd get down town and got into his car. He was thinking of the social security scheme. It had misfired, badly, and he couldn't understand why.

They'd had so much trouble, Farran had thought up this scheme to show labour he wasn't antagonistic to their interests. And yet it had recoiled on him. He knew the trouble was they were completely suspicious of him, they suspected double-dealing in everything he did. And he couldn't understand why.

The hell, he thought, stabbing for the starter button, he didn't give a damn about anything except putting his beloved planes out. Labour was welcome to the best they could get out of the deal, the best he could give them, with a bank holding most of the mortgages and ten thousand shareholders owning thirty-five per cent of the shares. But they wouldn't get the best with this series of wildcat strikes to strangle production. No one got the best out of such things.

He threw his car into a skid deliberately, passing the chuck wagon. The yawp was on another hamburger, sneering as he passed. The dust shot up quickly from the slipping wheels and got him nicely. Farran heard the crowd laugh to see him put one over so neatly on the big yawp. They always kept their humour, those boys, that was one good thing.

It put Farran in a good temper, and he took a look back. The yawp was saying things and trying to get the dirt off his hamburger.

Farran went to town. He didn't know what to do there, but he knew he couldn't do anything profitable out at the plant. That was a dead place and for the moment he was better out of it, leaving things to Labour Relations Officer Uncle El.

As he drove into Los Angeles, he kept wondering why a perfectly good scheme, designed to give the men security, should be so misinterpreted. But no sooner had he put up the idea than there'd been trouble — trouble somehow ending in a walkout.

They'd got the idea that the weekly deductions to pay for the scheme (though the firm put up half the money, in the end) was an attempt to cut their wages. It took some working out, thought Farran cynically, but that's how they'd got it in their heads. They argued that for years — on an average twenty years — the Farran concern would be having the use of part of their earnings. Multiplied by ten thousand it represented millions. They thought it was a swindle. And somehow, because they were touchy, they'd come out on strike.

But Farran thought, 'There's more to it than this,' but couldn't think what it was.

He gave the red coupé a lot of gas, going over the plain towards the screen of hills behind L.A. It was a pretty good car, as it should have been, because it had cost half a million to make.

It could do around a hundred and forty, so he'd been told, though he'd never tried to shove the needle up so far.

He liked to tool around at a modest pace; he wasn't in any hurry when he was on four wheels. Eighty suited him — or maybe an occasional ninety when there weren't any kinks in the road. But not speeding. He liked to do his speeding at least twenty thousand feet above sharp bends and traffic snarls.

Farran let the needle doodle around the eighty figure. Burt might be a sorehead, but he sure could design a car — given half a million or so.

It had been Burt's idea. Right after the war, when cancellation came in for combat planes and the mighty Farran plant stood nearly as empty as it was now, Brother Burt had come up with the scheme. Aviation, according to him was pretty well through. There'd be no more wars, and what chance had civil aviation alone of keeping this mighty plant going?

So he said, 'The world needs cars. They'll never get enough automobiles, because we're building roads now to burn 'em out within a couple of years. Okay, let's turn Farrans over to making good, fast autos,'

He even brought Henry Ford up to clinch the argument, though it was an argument in reverse. 'Ford turned from making cars to making planes, didn't he? What Ford can do that way, we can do oppositely.'

It had been his brainchild — and he had a good brain for designing though it wasn't geared to practical production techniques.

The baby took a long while to emerge. Maybe there was more to making a car than looked from the outside, as Henry Kaiser was also beginning to find. When a year had passed, and half a million in research was down the drain, Farran put a stop to the agony.

'We know how to make planes,' he said. 'Okay, we'll stick to making 'em. We'll gamble on the market picking up within a couple or three years and we'll go ahead with carrier planes.'

It had picked up. And but for these strikes they'd have been sitting pretty, too. The one prototype car made, hand-built down to the last nut and bolt, almost, was a beauty, though not to be bought at such a price ever again.

And it had done some good, because Burt wouldn't come near the factory now. Burt stayed home these days and sulked, because he hadn't been given the fifty million he'd found they'd need to get even a modest assembly line moving. He still got up ostentatiously when Farran came into the room, and stalked silently out.

Farran turned into the Boulevard some time later and thought that was one good thing, anyway, getting rid of Burt. The Farran plant was stiff with relatives, and he didn't give a darn for any of them. Not many, anyway.

He stopped off at Clem Cole's bar and had lunch, though the coffee didn't have the smell of that strong brew from the strikers' wagon and the hamburgers definitely lacked virility. Then he got back into his car and turned towards Santa Monica Harbour.

Maybe with this wind offshore he'd do some sailing. There wasn't anything else to do, and sailing did take your mind off bellyaches. And he'd got a nice boat all waiting for him.

Two blocks from Clem's he saw Lydia Van Heuson. She had come out of Macartneys and looked about to get a taxi. She was dressed to kill, and the moment she saw Farran she thought he was the answer.

Farran trailed his eyes away just as he saw Lydia's face brighten and her hand come up. Then he went right on past her, just as if she wasn't there. 'The hell, she can buy a taxi,' he thought. He'd been out with Lydia plenty times, and she wasn't for him any more. Not for a mind soured by a strike back over the hills costing half a million a week.

But it did something, seeing Lydia. He went right across, instead of coming left at the next intersection — even avoiding a woman brought you trouble. And that meant driving on to the next crossing and making the turn there.

In itself, with all those horses prancing under the bonnet, that was no hardship, but coming into the unaccustomed turn Farran remembered the name of the street — and a number.

He stopped on an impulse. This was

where Joe McMee had set up office a couple of months back — he'd promised to look him up and hadn't, and always when he remembered he'd felt a bit of a heel in consequence.

They'd been through college together, Joe McMee and Russ Farran. Joe had been a better boy in the lecture room than on the football field, and he'd only made the team in a few games, but Farran had got to know — and like — him during those times.

A good, steady, plodding type, Joe, yet curiously brilliant on occasions. A man of contradictory character, Farran thought. Joe had joined the F.B.I. when his degree came through, and for a few years was quietly out of everybody's ken.

Then he'd hit the headlines, digging out some of the Detroit Chopper Boys. In his curious way he had had his usual flash of brilliance and made good.

He'd spoken to Farran over the phone on making L.A. He'd quit the F.B.I. Farran felt the regret in his voice. He'd married, got a wife who thought there was no sense in taking risks.

'She's right,' Joe's slow, heavy voice had come over the wire to Farran. 'I got hurt with the Chopper Boys. Bad. And that's something you've always got to expect in the Bureau. Getting hurt, I mean.'

So, for his wife's sake, he'd quit the G-job and set up office here in L.A. No, he didn't call himself a detective, Joe told him modestly. Just an enquiry agent. Now, there must be a lot of things needed enquiring into at a place as big as Farrans . . .

Farran promised to look him up some time when he was in town, and turned him over to his Labour Relations Officer, who might find work for him. Farran hadn't thought to ask Uncle El how Joe had made out with him.

He got out of his car slowly. He didn't really want to meet Joe. Not while he was in this broody mood. They'd been pals at college, but friendships kind of died as the years of maturity piled up. Still, out of politeness, now he was in the district, he'd drop in on Joe. Perhaps Joe wouldn't be in, he thought hopefully. Then he'd be able to go sailing with an easy conscience.

He went up. Joe's office looked like any of the other hundreds in the same building. Just one door with his name in black across the glass — Joe McMee, Enquiry Agent. Farran walked through without knocking. It's a habit you get when you own hundreds of doors and you want to save seconds of time all day.

There was no one in the microscopic reception office, but Farran saw that the inner office door was slightly open, so he went straight on through the little swing gate and walked in on Joe McMee.

Joe was lying on his back, one foot stuck in a wire wastepaper basket. His chair was over on its side against the wall, and there were some — but not many — papers on the floor.

Farran stopped in the doorway, and was immediately impressed by the still-ness, the quietness of that office. Especially the stillness of Joe.

So he went cautiously a couple of paces into the room and saw then that Joe would never make another noise this side of wherever good Joes go.

A blue-rimmed hole made a startlingly

vivid mark on Joe's right temple, just where the hair was thinning back. A hole that could have been made by a spinning three-eight bullet. A hole that was big enough, in that place, to spill the life out of anyone.

Anyway, it had spilled the life out of big Joe McMee, enquiry agent.

2

Farran felt himself go as stiff as a tomcat scenting danger. And it felt, too, as though his hackles were risen on end. He looked at Joe, and looked and looked and went on looking. And back of his eyes his brain was spinning madly, trying to cope with a situation foreign to it.

Murder!

Because there was no gun in the dead man's hand, no gun anywhere near it. And men can't shoot holes in their temples like that without guns. Someone had done it for him.

Farran looked at the wastepaper basket on Joe's foot. It looked comical, made the dead Joe look funny. For the first moment, that is. Afterwards it looked somehow obscene, certainly indecent.

And Farran saw how it was. Those two paces into the room had brought him in view of a part-opened drawer — the top left drawer of, presumably, the late Joe

McMee's desk. Inside Farran saw a gun — it looked like a Colt, probably a four-five service weapon.

Could be Joe had made a dive for that drawer, got it part-opened before the death bullet tore through his skull. And in making that dive it looked as though Joe had stuck his foot into the basket — could be that basket had hindered him in going for his own gun, had delayed him just that vital fraction of time which had resulted in this. This — a scene over which only bells could toll.

Farran looked at a telephone on the desk. His blood was beginning to thaw out. He knew that a wise guy in a movie or the crime book of the month would walk out and solve the mystery; but he also knew that a wise guy in real life picked up the nearest telephone and bawled 'Police' until the place was stiff with blue uniforms.

He was a wise guy in real life, Farran, so he went over to use that phone.

Then he felt — it was really too soft to hear — a movement and he jerked his head round so quickly he heard his neck crick.

There was a girl huddled against the wall not a yard to his left. He just hadn't seen her because a corpse — especially the corpse of a man who had shared a blanket with you on a football bench — compels a whole lot of attention.

She was blonde and soft and young and probably pretty. But right now her face was whiter than the snows of Alaska, and her straining eyes were so big they looked as if something was shoving hard up behind them. There was an expression of dazed agony on that small, up-tilted face.

Farran looked and realised that though those eyes were fixed roughly in his direction they weren't focusing. The girl was looking, but she wasn't seeing much.

He forgot the phone for a minute. Afterwards he thought; 'The heck, that's just how it happens in a movie!' And then, of course, a big lug like Sydney Greenstreet smiles in at the doorway, beans you and rings for the police. They find you with a gun in your hand and everyone says, 'You done it, pal. Quit arguing, can't yer?' All except the heroine. There's always a heroine to believe — the heck, didn't Hollywood built itself up on Glamour?

But just at that moment Farran didn't think any of that. He quite naturally went and bent over the girl. His voice demanded, 'What's happened? Who are you? Who killed Joe?' Like that. He was good at firing questions, even if unions no longer made it possible for the boss to fire employees.

And the girl just said nothing.

She couldn't. Farran took a look behind her blonde head and decided the lump could have come from a bang against a wall. He was still so unprepared for criminal answers to problems that he didn't think someone might have bent a rod over the head instead.

He took hold of her under her arms. She was wearing a thin attractive summer dress. He lifted, and the head at first lolled back and he saw the bloodless lips part as a moan came through and then pain brought the swift movement of life and her head came forward and erect again. He held her, though she was all weight in his arms, and her face went tight with the agony of returning consciousness, and she looked to be fighting a rising tide of sickness.

Farran stuck her on the desk, still holding her. His eyes were on that phone again. He rapped, 'Sit up, can you? I've got some phoning to do.' Terse. There were a lot of women out at his plant on the edge of the desert; he was used to them about.

His words got through. The blonde made an effort and sat swaying feebly holding the edge of the desk with hands that, unusual for L.A., didn't have points to their fingers and colour on the nails. Her eyes were looking at Farran now, focusing.

Farran got the phone; put a call through to police. The girl listened. 'Someone's been killed . . . Yeah, I know his name — Joe McMee, ex-F.B.I.' That'd bring 'em up in their chairs. Cops didn't like death in the family, and G-men were cops. 'I'll wait,' he told them, and gave the address.

One minute later a prowl car must have got the radio and came screaming along the street outside. The L.A. cops weren't slouches.

The blonde was recovering fast. The eyes weren't out so much now She was slim, her face was almost thin. A nice face. Nothing special about it, just — nice. And there weren't many nice faces so near Hollywood; they were all too special for that.

She said, 'It is real?' and there were tears rolling down her cheeks faster than rain at a barbeque.

He said, 'About Joe? Getting shot?' He looked at the silent Joe, lying on his back with his foot inside the WPB. 'Yeah, I guess it's real.' And then he added, 'The G-man got his. Poor Joe.' He didn't get sentimental; he hadn't been brought up to be that way. But he didn't like to see a man who had been his friend lying like that. Killed. Murdered.

She went on weeping silently, her blue eyes caught on Farran's, as if she felt she was anchoring on to a strength she badly needed at that moment. When she spoke it was through lips that were nearly without movement, so that

Farran could hardly hear her.

'You knew Joe? Not many people knew he'd been a G-man.'

'Yeah. I knew Joe. We played football at college together.' He nearly added, 'I played; he sat most of the time on the benches.' Not quite as good. But he refrained; it wasn't necessary, and he had a vague idea it was even a bit irreverent.

The girl began to sway, and her eyes started to go a bit ga-ga. He caught her, steadied her, demanded, 'Who're you? Did you see it happen?'

She started to shake her head, then winced at a stab of pain. Her head began to droop forward as she spoke, so he kept hold of her. 'I came in.' That slow, tired whisper. She'd had enough, that girl. Too much. 'He was — just like that. Dead.' She was becoming heavier in his arms, her tired head almost touching his chest.

He asked again, 'Who are you? Come on, who are you?' Demanding, because he had asked the question three times now, and he wasn't used to asking a question more than once before getting an answer.

This time it came. Two words. 'His . . .
wife . . . '

She was all weight when a police
sergeant came shoving a face heavy with
suspicion round the door. There was
another cop with him, chewing. The
sergeant tried shock tactics.

He looked at Joe with his foot in the
basket, looked at Farran, holding Joe
McMee's unconscious widow. And he
said, 'You did it.' And it was no question.

Farran looked sour. Really sour. Sourer
than most men ever get even once in their
life. And when he came back with his
answer it zipped, tore holes into that fresh
cop. 'You say that again, and my
attorney'll go for your department for
slander.'

He didn't take talk from fresh guys, not
even cops.

The sergeant got it, that this tall, lean,
brown-faced hombre didn't let wise guys
go to play with him. He got more than
that — that this jaw-jutting, brittle-eyed
guy was someone, even in a State where
there were a lot of someones.

The cop with the chew paused, said,

'Dat guy's Farran. Him with all them airplanes, sarge.' Then went on chewing. And the accent wasn't Californian. Strictly Brooklyn — or to stretch a point, maybe Yonkers. East Coast, not West. But a dumb cop at that, even if he had recognised Farran.

The sergeant climbed down. 'I said, 'Who did it'?'

Farran grunted. The sergeant took a look round, then he did some grunting. 'They'll be along with an ambulance in a few minutes,' he said. 'Homicide.' Then he took a long gander at the corpse, as if it fascinated him.

Farran watched them, thinking it might be interesting to see professionals at work, but they never did a thing. Then there was the sound of a lot of sirens down in the street below, and a few moments later the room became solid with men all doing a job.

Mrs. McMee came to life again with all the noise, but she was still pretty sick, and Farran found she was holding on to his arm very tightly for support. He sat up on the desk beside her and held her. After a time she realised what he was doing and he heard her say, 'Thanks . . . I feel — bad.'

Farran looked over her shoulder at big Joe. He thought, 'Now, what do you do in such situations?' He had to think things out, because when you are bred to millions it's usually other people who have to be considerate. But he got an idea very soon.

'Look, you'd better get away from — him,' he told her. 'I'll take you out into the passage.' It wasn't good for a girl to be sitting almost on top of a husband — deceased. He helped her off the desk and got her across the room.

The cop who chewed was leaning on the door. He said, 'You don't go out. Nobody goes out. I got orders.'

Farran stood there, holding the girl. 'You fetch me the guy that gives those orders,' he told him toughly.

A police lieutenant came across. He was quite a pleasant guy. He'd been told who the girl was. 'You want to get her out of this atmosphere, of course,' he said. 'Yes, take her outside. There's a settee along at the end by the elevator. I'll come in a few minutes and get a statement from you.'

There were some nice cops, thought Farran, sitting by the whining elevator. Then he saw that the gum-chewer had lounged near and was watching them, and he thought, 'Nice, but they don't take chances where murder's concerned.'

The girl started off by holding her head between her hands, and then she got a little better and sat up and looked at Farran.

He said, in that blunt way of his, 'That was a shock to you. All that.' He didn't soften his voice or try to express sympathy. It didn't occur to him; he wasn't built that way. Some time later he realised a remarkable thing — that the girl didn't want sentiment, didn't want gestures of sympathy.

In some curious way she understood his manner at once — accepted it and appreciated it.

'Yes,' she said just now. 'It was — a shock.' Her blue eyes were looking into immeasurable distances, all covering horror. They turned to Farran, looked at him. 'You won't leave me?' she whispered.

Farran looked away to consider the request. 'That's asking something, isn't it?' he said at length. 'Why me? Haven't you got relatives or friends hereabouts?'

'Not here. In New York.' Her face was troubled. 'That's a long way, and — well, they're not the kind to come distances.'

'So you're on your own?'

'Now Joe's gone — yes.'

She began to cry again. Farran thought it might be a feminine device, even if unconscious, to arouse his sympathy. All the same he didn't think the worse of her for that, because he had imagination — men who design aircraft must have — and he could project himself some way into the appalling situation she so suddenly found herself in.

'I reckon at a time like this you do feel you've got to have someone around to talk to.' He told her who he was. 'Farran. Russ Farran. I build planes. Good ones. I *did*,' he thought bitterly, remembering that strike picket at the gates of the mighty Farran works.

'I know about you. Joe mentioned you sometimes.' And then the lieutenant came and separated them and took individual statements. When that was done, and the police doctor had examined the girl's head (to corroborate her story, that she had fainted and struck her head in falling, Farran thought cynically), the police lieutenant told them they could go. He said it very pleasantly, but he also added that they shouldn't leave the city boundaries because he might want to contact them again at any time.

Farran took the girl down. When they went out into the white, late afternoon sunshine, it seemed to hit up from the sidewalk and sent the girl's head spinning again, so he steered her into a café and ordered strong coffee for her. His theory was that strong coffee was good for a hangover; okay, what was the difference between a hangover and a bump on the head? Just one big pain in either case.

The coffee did her good, too. She looked at it, got the strong smell up her nostrils, and shuddered. She didn't touch it, but she got over her giddiness pretty quickly, so it could have been the coffee smell that helped.

It wasn't very crowded, but they couldn't talk because the tables were on close, friendly terms with each other, and they didn't want the fat guy back of them to hear what might be said.

So after a time they rose and walked out. The girl seemed to lead, as if running away from something. Farran came after her because he knew she needed watching until she could settle down again.

She turned and walked down towards the harbour road. The street was pretty quiet, but it was too hot in that white Californian sunshine for walking. Yet she seemed to want to walk.

Farran humoured her as far as the end of the street, where the busy harbour road intersection was, and then he took her arm and said, 'You've got to pull yourself together. Lady, you're almost sleepwalking now. I was on my way sailing, but I can find time to drop you off some place if you want me to.'

His brusque manner did her good, jolted her back to the present. She turned towards him, that white face too white to be pleasing, those blue eyes too big with shock to be attractive. And yet Russ Farran again had that feeling that she was a nice girl; there was some quality about her that appealed to him . . . something he didn't usually notice in the butterflies who fluttered round his bachelor life.

He heard her whispered voice — 'You tell me what to do. I can't think. I'm still trying to work out something awful.'

His eyebrows lifted.

'I'm a widow.' Her slight shoulders shrugged. 'A very new widow. I can't get over the shock. What's it going to mean to my life to be a widow? Without Joe. My Joe!'

He grabbed her quickly as she halted and swayed. Suddenly he was touched by the grief in her voice — here was one girl who loved her husband. He thought perhaps that was why he found her vaguely attractive to him; most of the girls he knew didn't love their husbands if they had any and wouldn't love them when they got them. And 'them' wasn't a careless choice of word with the Lydia

Van Heusons in that part of America.

He soothed her down. Anyone watching him, as there was, would have looked at his rough, unpractised gestures in that light.

He patted her shoulder a few times, then stroked her back until he realised that was no thing to do to a lady. And all the time he was saying things like, 'C'mon, you've got to keep living. Okay, make the best of it — just stop thinking for a coupla months and then let yourself wake up gradually.'

It did her good, again. If he had softened his voice and spoken sympathy she would have broken down, but as it was he gave her no opportunity to indulge in self-sympathy.

'Where shall I take you?' They were walking back towards his car. He thought, anyway, he wasn't over-bothered about sailing. That was just to get his mind off the silent, nearly empty Farran works.

She shrugged her slim shoulders again. 'I don't know. Don't care. I know I don't want to go home for a while.' She looked quickly at him, pleading with her eyes for understanding. 'It's a little place — a two-roomed apartment. It'll be — full of Joe. You know what I mean. Reminding me. And Joe was a — was a . . . ' She couldn't end it.

'A fine guy.' Farran supplied the tail to the epitaph; it wasn't inspired but it was sufficient. 'Okay, keep away from your apartment for some time. Maybe don't go back there again ever.' He thought for a moment. 'I know a good place in the country — you know, flowers and fields and trees. It'd set you up again, maybe.'

She was looking across the road, shaking her blonde head slowly. 'I don't know where I want to go. I — I'm afraid of loneliness. We felt pretty lonely as it was, coming to this strange town. But without Joe — ' She was near to breaking down.

It was a problem. Farran solved it. 'Maybe you'd better move out to my place. We've hundreds of rooms. I suppose.' He wondered how she would get on with Elsa and the rest of the family, but decided it might work out all right. The family only gunned for him,

Russ Farran, who had inherited the Farran Empire.

'That's nice of you.' Her blue eyes were searching his face. 'You'd do me good, you know, being near me.' It shook him a bit. She went on, 'You don't fuss and say the right things — the right things that right people say, that is. You — you brace me when you talk. I'd like to come out to your place. Won't I be in the way, though?' There was a wistful uncertainty in her voice.

He spoke truthfully; he always did, which was why he had few friends but they were very good ones. 'Guess I'll have work to do, but maybe I'll be able to help with things.' He was wondering how girl-widows like this were able to cope with inquests and funerals and setting about the job of starting to live again. 'You won't see much of me, but Elsa — she's my stepmother — can be quite friendly in her way.'

He started to reach out for the door handle, but the girl said, 'Keep walking. I want to make — sure.'

It startled him but he found himself

going on up the street. He heard the girl say, 'I learned a lot from Joe. He was a very smart G-man in his day.'

'We've passed my car,' he reminded her. At that she turned very quickly; he caught up with her and they went back to his car.

Then she told him they were being followed. She said it as though it was a shock to her.

Farran took a quick look along the sidewalk, but he didn't see any tail or anyone who looked as though he could be tailing them. So he said so.

The girl said, 'You're not looking in the right places. No good tail ever walks behind you — only in movies. He's always across the road from you. Look.'

She pointed to where a big guy with too much in his pants-seat was suddenly being interested in a ladies' underwear display. A really big guy, who would have looked more at home staring at fight bills or a horseracing programme.

Farran helped her into his car and started up. 'Why's he tailing us?' He was an aircraft manufacturer, not a 'tec, and he didn't know any of the answers. The girl didn't know many, either.

She shrugged. Both were sneaking glances across the road out of their eye corners. As Farran pulled out they saw the big guy whistle in a cab and come after them.

Farran went down towards the harbour, then turned south. If it came to a chase he didn't think that cab was going to hold him for long, not with this half-million bucks' worth of metal beneath him.

But Farran wasn't the kind to run away without knowing why he was doing it. He let the cab keep close behind until they came to a flower-ornamented roundabout in the suburbs. Then he gave it the gun and went round the circle at a dizzy speed. The taxi tried gallantly for a second, then fell rapidly behind. A quarter of a minute later and Farran was tailing the cab.

It gave the show away. Their tail knew now he had been spotted, but for a full half minute he didn't know what to do, so the cab went on chasing madly round the roundabout with Farran hooting derisively ten yards in the rear. Finally the tail must have told the cabbie to pull out on to the Farranville road, and it cut across the thin traffic stream that hadn't appreciated all this manoeuvring and crawled away.

Farran drove it into the side of the road and made it stop. The girl grabbed him as he started to climb out. 'What are you going to do?'

'Bust his flat pan for him,' snarled Farran. 'I don't like being followed — not by apes like that.'

But she clung to him and her voice was urgent, 'Be careful — don't you see, this might be someone who shot Joe!'

That thought hadn't occurred to him. He just wasn't built for detective work, he decided.

He said, 'Yeah, it's an idea. But bustin' up his face could still go into the programme.'

The big ape was taking the cab to bits in an effort to come quickly through the door. Farran was there right in front of him when he came out.

44

'I'm going to pretty up your profile unless you have a sound reason for tailing me,' Farran began, and his fist was hard back ready to start travelling.

The big ape looked at him from eyes that had been punched back a couple of inches into his thick skull. He mouthed. 'I'm too big a boy ter start fightin' with strangers,' and he pulled a gun on Farran.

3

The cabbie looked on approvingly. He was a wise guy. All cabbies, anyway, are just the wisest guys. He deadpanned, 'You dive fer his gun, mister. You dive so fast he don't have a chance to pull trigger.'

The ape with the gun said, 'Shaddup. Look, Mister Farran, I don't want any trouble with you, but as sure as I was given this gun to use, so help me I'll use it if you try being smart, see?'

'You know me?'

'Guess I'd know you even if I didn't work for the police department.'

Farran's hands didn't come down at that because he had forgotten to put them up. He realised that the girl had run up behind him and was standing very close to his side.

'A cop?' Farran began to understand.

'You're psychic.' He looked like primitive man but Farran was realising that the ape carried a slick brain behind that battered pan. And he had a mild sense of humour, apparently.

Farran squared up to him. 'But why are you tailing me?'

And then the idea jumped into his mind that perhaps they weren't tailing him at all, they were tailing Joe McMee's widow. The thought was ugly and he didn't linger with it.

The ape shrugged. The movement didn't carry to his gun hand. That hand was so steady it was astonishing. It was the first time Farran had ever been made to look into the mouth of a Colt, but he found he wasn't caring much for the novelty that is supposed to go with new experience.

'I do as I'm told, Mr. Farran.'

'So you intend to go on tailing me?'

'You,' corrected the ape, and the word embraced the girl. Farran heard her gasp ever so slightly.

'Okay.' Once he knew it didn't bother Farran. 'You won't be able to keep pace with me across to Farranville in that old can.' The cab driver looked sour; maybe he owned the vehicle. 'You'll find us both at my home — and everyone knows where that is in Farranville.'

He grabbed the girl and hustled her into his car, then drove like fury so that the taxi never had a chance. Farran was damned if he was going to have a cop on his tail then or ever.

Entering the broad, tree-lined avenues that his father had built when he moved his airplane works to California, Farran slowed to a mere forty. He wanted to say a few things to this girl.

'You know why he is on our tail?'

'He thinks perhaps I killed my husband.' The girl took it calmly.

Farran had thought beyond that. 'The police wouldn't be surprised to find we had done it — you and I.'

'You and I?' She turned towards him, her face incredulous. The drive had whipped colour into her cheeks. She looked quite a good-looking girl now — still not exotic, but none the worse for that. 'But why should they think we would do that?'

'Wives have conspired to have unsuspecting husbands removed before today.

How're they to know? It's their job to find out, and that's why they're tailing us.' He shrugged. 'It kind of burns me up a bit, but — it's their job.'

He drove towards that mighty Farran house up on the green, tree-clad slopes back of Farranville. Abruptly he asked, 'You didn't kill him? Joe, I mean. Did you?'

'No.' She shook her head. 'A lot of people will be thinking that question, won't they? I suppose it's natural.'

Then she came back with a surprising question. 'Did you?'

'Good God, no.' He steered into the long driveway. 'Have you been thinking that?'

'Only just now, when you asked that question. I suddenly thought, you were in that office when I came to. Perhaps you had been there all the time.'

'But you don't believe it of me, do you?'

'No — but you'll have trouble with the police.'

He stopped the car at that, pulled in behind the last screen of bushes before the house.

'Hadn't you thought of that?' She was watching him, seemed sorry for him, which was curious coming from her.

'No.' Funny, but it hadn't occurred to him.

She said wearily, 'I suppose being married to a G-man means that I have learned a lot of the police mind. I have a feeling you are police suspect No. 1 right now.'

'But why?'

'Probably because they can't think of anyone else.' She sounded tired. 'I'm sorry, I seem to be bringing trouble on you. Look, take me somewhere — to an hotel, maybe. Coming to stay with you might only make things more unpleasant for you.'

'I see.' Farran thought, 'She means it'll get me in deeper. Okay, let it get me in as deep as it likes.'

A sudden fury seemed to grip him. These days nothing went smoothly for him, nothing went right. Okay, he hadn't been sticking out his neck before, but maybe this time he'd try it for a change. Yeah, he'd stick his neck out, even though there was a cop with a nightstick ready to crack it for him.

'You're going to stay up here, Mrs. McMee,' he growled obstinately. 'I don't let anyone shove me around. If the cops get tough, okay, I'll get tough. And I've got a few million to fight 'em with. Maybe I'll enjoy fightin' the cops — it'll be something to occupy my mind while there's no work for me down at the factory.'

But she shook her head, spoke and quieted him like a hotheaded boy reproved by a gentle-voiced teacher. 'It's bad to fight cops. They're working to help us — in my case to find a murderer. I'd rather help than fight them.'

'Sorry.' He started up again. 'I didn't quite mean it that way. I'll fight only if they try to put anything across on me.'

She spoke just as they were pulling up before the huge house on the hill crest, a house that owed something to the Greeks and a lot more to an architect with a Deep South training — it had a wide front of Ionic pillars, long, shuttered windows and high-ceilinged rooms, and it was as cold as the Arctic in winter.

'I don't like to be called Mrs. McMee by you. Can't you use my first name?'

He helped her out. 'If I know it.'

'It's the funniest name. You've never heard it before, not for a first name.' She looked at him doubtfully. 'It's got me into a lot of trouble — people make fun if it. My Christian name's . . . Darling.'

'Darling?' Some overfed monkey opened the door to them. 'That's a queer name, isn't it?'

'It was my father's idea. He didn't have very good ones.'

'Some of my father's weren't so bright,' consoled Farran and he was looking in on the family tearing each other to pieces right there and then in the main lounge.

Not Elsa, of course. She sat in her hair net, with a wrap tied round her bulging, past-middle-aged figure. She reminded Farran of a queen ant, these days surrounded always by her many children, his half-brothers and half-sisters.

Burt was there, though he got up the moment he saw Farran in the door, and most obviously left the room. Burt was the eldest of his 'halfs,' four years his junior and not grown up at all. He'd go away now and sulk in his room. Farran shrugged.

Arnold and Lew went on with a row that never ended while the pair were together — Arnold with his handkerchiefs up his sleeve and his affectations and superciliousness; Lew aping the crudest of college behaviour, with his crew cuts and show-off clothes.

And back of them Rita making up her petulant little face June, saying catty things about her dress and figure, and even seventeen-year old Alyss shooting barbs when she could be bothered to lift her face out of *Life*.

Nobody took any notice of them as they stood in the doorway, so Farran finally said, ironically, 'This is home.'

Her reaction was curious; it came swiftly, unexpectedly. 'Why do you put up with it? You can afford to live elsewhere, can't you?'

'Sure.' He eyed the squabbling family with distaste. 'I think I hang on out of habit. It's convenient, living here almost on top of the works.'

That was usually all that mattered, being near to the big factory that bore his name. He wasn't home much, and the family could go hang when they were out of his sight.

Still, there were times when he wondered if it was a good thing, living with his father's second wife and her children. She wasn't a bad sort, Elsa. She'd nursed his father through an illness after the death of his first wife, and when he'd decided he couldn't live without her she had done as he ordered and married him.

She'd been a good wife to him, too. Farran never denied that. She'd also been vaguely kind and good to Farran Senior's first and only child, Russ. Maybe that was why Russ Farran tolerated the family, though the house, like the Farran Empire, had all been left to him. He didn't want to upset Elsa by getting tough with her family, though they deserved a lot . . .

Farran started to take the girl across to the big stairway. Nobody moved for him, and it made him sour. They all resented the fact that he had inherited the Farran Empire.

They all had jobs of some sort down in the works, but they were drones and passengers and didn't earn their keep. And they all thought they could do better than the man who had stepped into his father's shoes.

Elsa looked up, her fat face unpleasant with foundation cream. 'I get so tired,' she wailed to her stepson. 'I was going out but I got tired before I finished dressing, so you'll have to excuse my wrap.'

But that was said for the benefit of this pale-faced, straight-built girl with Farran. Elsa was always getting tired and wandering around inside a wrap. But she meant well.

Farran kept right on through the family, so Elsa called, 'Who's that, Russ? Shouldn't you introduce us — or something?' — vaguely.

Over his shoulder Farran said, just as vaguely, 'She's my widow. I'm taking care of her.' And at that Elsa looked round and then said to no one in particular, 'But that isn't possible. Is it?'

Alyss threw down *Life* and smiled as he came up. Alyss had done a lot of smiling at him in the last few weeks, he suddenly remembered, though she'd been as pert and hostile towards him as the rest of the family, previously. He thought perhaps the smiles were preparation for advancement at the works. She had elected to leave college at an early age and go into Social Welfare at Farrans, and alone of the family she seemed interested in her work.

Alyss said, "Lo, Russ. You should be down at the factory.'

He stared at her. 'Come again?'

'Didn't Uncle El tell you? About the strike breakers?' She was a bright kid, and nice when she wasn't imitating her family. 'Uncle El's going to try to bust the strike by bringing in imported labour.'

Farran said, dispassionately, 'Uncle El's so far mad he should be shot if he's really got that idea in his fat head.' And he couldn't believe it.

Alyss shrugged and dropped the subject. She was looking with interest at

56

the girl — and Darling McMee was about tuckered in at that moment.

'You don't look well.' Alyss suddenly took hold of the girl's hands, and there was something practised and professional about the movement that she had learned on her job with Social Welfare.

Farran said, jerkily, 'She's had a shock. Her husband . . . murdered.' Alyss's eyes widened, then she gripped more firmly. 'I thought she could live around with us as she doesn't want to go to her apartment or to an hotel.'

'Why, of course. Look, Russ, you've done as much as you can do.' Alyss took command of the situation very well.

He thought, 'None of the others would behave like this,' and was in fact surprised to find his half-sister so suddenly efficient.

'She'll want me to go fetch her things, I suppose. You leave her to me, I'll look after her.'

Farran was relieved. He said, 'That's good of you, Alyss.' Then he introduced them. 'This is Alyss, my sister. Meet Mrs. McMee.' He found humour somewhere inside him. 'You won't believe it, but her first name's Darling — Darling McMee.'

He started to turn away, though he had nothing to do, nowhere to go. Then Alyss, arm linked through Darling's, now said urgently, 'Look, Russ, can't you just go down to the factory? I mean, Uncle El's plan . . .'

He jerked into rigid amazement, 'The heck, Alyss, you're not serious, are you? Uncle El would be mad to bring labour in with that mob at the gate. That's not the way to settle labour problems.' He just couldn't believe it; at one time El Farran had had the highest reputation for being a labour mediator.

Alyss shrugged her plump young shoulders, then started to help Darling McMee up the stairs. The blonde girl paused, a few steps up; her blue eyes sought Farran's — they smiled ever so faintly. And he knew that was her thanks.

He crossed the lounge again, patted his stepmother affectionately but ignored the rest of her brood, who just as pointedly ignored him. As he got into his car he was thinking of the young blonde widow. He thought what a crude repellent word 'widow' was; somehow, even though it might be technically accurate, it didn't seem to apply to a young girl like Darling McMee.

When he came to the car park at the entrance to the works he realised that something was very much wrong at the Farran factory.

The riot squad from Los Angeles was there, though it had evidently just arrived in. The wide space in front of the gates was like a battleground, with five or six hundred strikers bawling their heads off and running around looking for something to hit.

The cops didn't have that problem. They were beating in at the nearest strikers around the gateway, their sticks fetching blood, and then a police lieutenant tossed a few tear gas bombs where the wind would take the acrid vapour down among the main mass of strikers without affecting his men at the gate.

Farran wasn't a fool and didn't stop out in the car park. He came whizzing in up to the gates very quickly, and the gateman saw him coming and got one gate wide enough open for him to bring his car through.

As he switched off he heard the shout of hate that rose from the strikers outside, and realised with a shock it was directed towards him. He got out and went up to the fence and looked upon hating, malignant, fury-distorted faces — hundreds of them. The mob swirled and broke through the first thin line of police and came charging towards the gate.

The lieutenant slipped through, shouting to his men to come back into safety. A shower of heavy stones and lumps of wood smacked against the wire-mesh fence that ran all around the works, but they did no harm to the people inside the factory.

The lieutenant didn't have the apparent friendliness of his brother officer down town. In fact he was distinctly short with the owner of Farrans'.

'Get out of sight,' he called. 'You're inflaming them by your presence.'

'Get out of sight? Me?' Farran's reply

was characteristic. 'What'n hell do you think I am? I own this place.'

The cop squared toughly up to him; he wasn't the kind to be impressed by a few hundred millions. 'You won't own anything if that mob get in at you. C'mon, move!'

The strikers were up at that fence now, whistling and shrieking their hate, and they looked ugly — Farran could believe the cop lieutenant when he said that his life was in danger.

'Okay,' he said resignedly, 'I'll keep out of sight. But I'm damned if I know why I should scuttle and run.'

The lieutenant heaved a tear gas bomb over the fence, said cryptically, 'Don't you? Think again, brother, maybe you'll remember.' He went away too quickly for Farran to say anything.

There was a lot of brawling going on, especially at the gate, but the tear gas sent them all streaming away in time. It didn't make the mob feel any pleasanter, and from a window up in the Administration Block Farran could feel that the hate was all coming his way.

He was no angel with his temper any time, but right now it grew foul. He had a feeling of bafflement; he was up against something he didn't understand, he felt. For months now it had been obvious that his workers just hated his guts — didn't trust him an inch. And he couldn't see why.

True he wasn't the kind of boss who fraternises — he didn't go and buy drinks at the Farran clubhouse or pitch a ball just to show what a democratic guy they had over them. He had his own interests and he went his own way. That, surely, wasn't sufficient to set his men against him, was it?

Or was it?

He thought he'd go see Uncle El to find out the position regarding the strike. Then he remembered those words he had refused to accept from Alyss — that Uncle El was running strike busters into the factory.

It halted him, remembering. After all, if Uncle El had done such a damned foolish thing it would account for the tide of hate at the gateway. He couldn't believe a

Labour Relations officer would be so stupid, however, but all the same he went on down to his uncle's department.

And again he went in without knocking.

Andilla was there, Art Andilla who represented the bank in affairs with Farrans. So was Coulsen who spoke for the recently formed Shareholders Association. And Bennett and Lodge, two of Farran's seven directors.

And Secretary to the company and Labour Relations Officer Uncle El — Uncle El the big shot, the high-powered tycoon . . . when he got the chance.

Andilla was speaking as Farran came barging in, though he stopped the second he saw Farran. The men glanced at each other and then continued silent.

Farran got it. A hostile meeting, for some reason discussing him. His hackles rose; he couldn't fight ten thousand, union-consolidated workers, but he could go for the men before him if they wanted a scrap.

'You wouldn't be talking about me?' he said bluntly, looking round from one to the other.

They kept their eyes away from his, but they looked hard and tight-lipped and . . . hostile.

Farran said, 'What is it now? And what's making those monkeys dance outside the cage?'

His audience glanced quickly at Uncle El, as if silently electing him spokesman. So Uncle El made appropriate clearing noises in his fat throat, shoved up his thick-lensed glasses and spoke.

'You shouldn't have said you were going to bring strike busters in, Russ. If you'd known anything about labour relations you'd have known that was asking for trouble. I can't do a thing while you interfere like this.'

Farran looked at that fat, yellow-leather face growling up at him, waited until the voice strangled off into silence somewhere in the fleshy stomach of the Labour Relations Officer, then said, 'Someone's crazy. More than crazy. I never said I was going to bring strike busters in — '

'But you're thinking about it?' That was Andilla, very quick and lawyer-like, watching him keenly to make sure he got no false answer.

'Not even thinking about it,' declared Farran. 'I've got a Labour Relations Officer, and I keep my nose out of such things. You tell him, Uncle El.'

But Uncle El didn't say anything, and Farran knew that here was another audience that simply didn't intend to believe anything he said. So he stalked across to where he could cover them all with his hard, angry eyes, and he demanded, 'Who says I've got such ideas? I heard they were yours, Uncle El.'

'Mine?' A rasp could have made a more musical note. 'What do you mean, Russ?'

'Alyss said you were planning to run scabs into the factory.'

'Alyss is nuts.' Not for the first time Farran wished he could see those eyes behind the thick, screening lenses; he had a feeling that he never knew what was in his uncle's mind and sometimes he wished he did. 'Where'd she get that tale?' snapped the heavy, bloodless lips of his relative.

Farran shrugged. 'Where did you get

the tale about me?'

Uncle El glanced across at Andilla, the bank representative. 'If you send ultimata to strike leaders . . . ' His heavy shoulders shrugged away responsibility for the consequences.

So Farran got good and mad because they were still talking in circles and getting nowhere. He thumped the desk and made everything dance on it, and. then he thumped it again because he found the first blow pleased something savagely destructive somewhere inside his frustrated soul.

'For Pete's sake, tell me quick and not in riddles. What's this about ultimata to the strikers?'

'They got a letter — typed but with your signature attached. It said that if the strike didn't end by the morning you proposed to dismiss your former employees and recruit from Los Angeles. It said that you intended to settle this strike your way — by busting it.'

Farran looked from one to the other, his head nodding slightly, the picture of sourness. 'And you and those hicks out there swallowed that story? How long have I been a screwball, for you to think I'd do anything like that?'

Andilla got up. 'That's what your uncle's been saying in your defence, Farran. However, your story doesn't hold in one important respect — I saw that letter myself on my way in, and I'm telling you that was your signature attached to it.'

'We'll get that letter.' Farran suddenly realised that he couldn't get it himself, not with that mob thirsting for blood. 'I never wrote any such letter — it's a frame up of some kind, though I don't see who's to gain by it.'

Not a man lifted his eyes to Farran's while he was speaking. They couldn't have said plainer, 'We don't believe a word you're saying, brother,' and he knew it.

Then Andilla got on to another subject. He was plenty tough for a natty, city-dressed man, but then he represented over a million million dollars.

'We held a meeting at my office in town, Farran, this morning.' His gesture embraced all but heavy, silent Uncle El. 'In fact we've held several meetings lately.'

Farran stared. Then he made a little imperative gesture with his hand and said, 'Come on, out with it. What about? Me? Farrans?'

'You — and Farrans.' He never liked Andilla, never liked any of the big financial people whom his uncle revered. But he'd always felt that Andilla was a straight man for all that and wouldn't pull any fast ones with him.

Andilla clasped his well-manicured hands and looked straight at him. 'We're beginning to think you're a jinx. Farran. We're beginning to think that our money isn't safe with Farrans while you are the boss. We decided this morning to call an Extraordinary General Meeting.'

'Why?'

'To decide if you can continue as head of Farrans.'

Farran flared, 'This business was left to me by the man who made it — my father. It's mine — '

Andilla said, 'Not on your life. You have

shareholders — '

'Who own only thirty-five per cent of stock.' It was becoming a battle between them. 'I own the rest, and while I own it I stay as boss.'

Andilla wasn't beaten. Financial gents never are. He smoothed his carefully clipped moustache and said, levelly, 'My bank will have something to say about that. We have big investments with Farrans, and we don't intend to stand by and see them lose value because the boss can't get on with the workforce. Bluntly, Farran, you must go. If you don't go we'll pull back our money and sink you.'

Farran looked at him and knew he would do it — do just as he said and ruin him. That kind didn't let emotional values enter into business at all.

He walked across to the door. 'You can call your extra-ordinary meeting. I'll be there — fighting. Something stinks around here, though I can't quite place it yet.' He let his eye trail from one heavy-jowled, beglassed face to another. He thought they all looked like Uncle El, all looked like what people thought big tycoons looked like. All except the real big tycoon, Art Andilla, who looked more like a well-to-do shirt-maker than anything.

'Yeah, I'm just beginning to realise there's a nasty smell around the place. Someone's trying to shove me off my seat, isn't that it, huh?' His voice was soft but it wasn't pleasant for all that. Only Uncle El looked up and let him see that dead-codfish pair of eyes of his that told him nothing.

His thoughts flew back to that idle thought that morning, when he'd been standing up over the flying wings in the airframe shop. It came back to him now. There was just too much labour trouble at the works for it to be uninspired.

'Someone's trying to get me in jake. I'm being given the push. If someone can fake a letter — '

'I don't think you'll prove that letter I saw was a fake.' That was Andilla, voice ironic. And he believed what he was saying, Farran felt that.

'It was a fake. Either that or I wrote it when I was drunk or drugged, and I don't remember ever being either. I wonder what other slanders or libels have been put out to dirty my name with labour?'

Uncle El suddenly remembered and said, 'The meeting's next Monday. Three clear days are needed according to our articles; that means five before we can mail out the letters.'

Farran stood in the door, his jaw stuck out pugnaciously. 'The heck, hold it when you're ready. I'll be there.'

Uncle El called him back almost as he went out of the doorway. 'Russ.'

'Well?'

Those thick lenses reflected light across at him as the head lifted quickly. Then the fat, bloodless lips drooled out a toneless question.

'You're being watched for murder, aren't you, Russ?'

It shook Farran, and its effect on the other men was atomic. Lodge rapped, 'What're you talking about, El?'

But Bennet said quickly, 'Farran, what'n hell have you been up to now?' — as if it wouldn't surprise him, anyway.

Farran walked back, his eyes sombre as he held that fishy gaze behind the glasses.

'What do you mean, and where did you get your information?'

Uncle El went on looking at him. 'I'm in with most public relations officers. Police headquarters came right through to me to check on you.'

'Check?' Farran's fists bunched. 'Such as what?'

'Did I know if you had any girl friends. One in particular — a married woman with an unusual name.' That fat, heavy face glanced towards his companions. 'I won't mention her name — maybe you know.'

'You mean . . . Darling McMee?' Farran didn't bother about ultra-politeness just then. He seethed; things were getting more unpleasant than he had imagined. 'What did you say?'

'I said nothing to harm you,' declared the fat man levelly. 'I said you knew her — '

'What makes you think that?'

'Don't you?' Surprise in that voice. 'You said her husband was an old friend when you sent him to me. I assumed — '

'That I knew her.' Farran had that

feeling of frustration and bafflement again. Things could go wrong where he was concerned, and yet he couldn't put his finger on the cause of it all. What Uncle El had assumed was what any man in a similar position would have assumed. 'Well, for your information, I didn't know her. Not until this afternoon. Then her dead husband introduced me to her.'

Uncle El blinked behind his glasses and said something about not knowing. The others kept looking covertly from one to the other.

Lodge said, 'They think you killed this friend of yours because of some affair with his wife?'

Farran laughed shortly. 'You're telling me. I don't know what they think. Honestly, it hadn't occurred to me anyone could think that.' He'd just walked in out of the blue to say hello to an old buddy, and all this came up and hit him in the face. 'There's a jinx on me all right,' he said grimly.

'Did you?' Lodge never was a fellow for tact.

Coulsen decided to come into the conversation just then. He was in a bit of a panic. He lived for his shareholders and all he could see now was a threat to their interests.

'Look, Farran, you've got to get away from this place. You can't stay on as head of Farrans while this sort of talk is being bandied about, I mean, things are bad between you and the work people already; when they get to know about this private affair, it'll be the limit, I'm telling you.' He mopped his bald head in agony. 'Resign — quit — leave Farrans to somebody else,' he blurted out finally.

Farran looked at the floor. There was no fierce anger in him now. He felt that what had frustrated him before because it had been so vague and intangible was now taking shape and he could begin to see and understand it. And understanding, he could start to think about it and fight back.

So he said, after a pause, 'I'm not resigning. I'm not going to permit any crafty bunch of schemers to push me out into the cold — '

Andilla's voice was chill. 'Are you suggesting that we are the crafty bunch of schemers, Farran?'

'I'm not suggesting anything,' said Farran flatly, but he didn't deny the idea. 'All I know is — someone's trying to get control of this business. Someone's trying to shove me out and doing it mighty cunningly. Someone's been queering my pitch for a long time, come to think of it. Well, I'm still in the game and fighting.'

Andilla's voice came with contempt in it. 'You're not seriously suggesting that someone's gone so far as to get you framed for murder?'

'I guess that's just my bad luck, that happening now.' Farran shrugged. 'And who says I'm going to be taken in for murder, anyway? I found the body; no one's got anything against me.'

'Only that unwittingly I gave the police to believe that you and the murdered man's wife were friends. I'm sorry I misled them, Russ.' Uncle El apologised like a gravel pit sounding sorry for itself. Then he growled on, 'You don't happen to know where she is now, do you?'

75

Farran came back from the door once again. His eyes were glinting savagely. 'Yeah, I took her home with me. Now what do you make of that, you and the cops?'

Then he went out, and it was only on his way to the gate that he began to wonder why his uncle had asked that question, anyway.

The police rode out in a tight cordon around him. They got out easily, picking a fortunate moment just when the mobile food bar pulled in. As Farran drove past he had a momentary impression of a man coming away, first from the head of the queue.

That big yawp with the sagging belly over his belt.

And the big yawp was watching him go by and wasn't saying anything bright this time. Much more curiously, he wasn't eating his hotdog, and hotdogs don't stay hot overlong and aren't any good when they go cold.

The cordon left him half way into town and returned to the works. Farran drove up to the front of the house, his brain trying to pick up some loose end that he could hold on to and then begin to unravel the knotty problem. But he couldn't. All he could think of was that a mighty business worth two hundred million bucks in the world of stocks and shares might be taken away from him by the slick, well-groomed representative of the bank whose money they used.

But he wouldn't lose the Farran Empire without a fight — without one hell of a fight, he thought, walking out of the garage.

He saw a shadow in the gloom of swift descending night. He came suddenly upon it as he started round towards the front of the colonial mansion that the Deep South architect had designed for his father.

He said, laconically, 'Come in, ape. You'll be cold out here.' And he and the ape went inside for a drink.

He thought, climbing into bed, later, it had been some day. To be threatened with a loss of a two hundred million dollar business and suspected of possible murder.

While he slept the ape proceeded carefully and methodically to read through all the correspondence he could find in Farran's private suite of rooms. And he seemed to find a few interesting things — things worth photostating . . .

4

When Farran came down to the breakfast room next morning, none of the family was there. But then none of the family ever got up for breakfast.

Elsa would have it brought to bed hours later, and so would petulant, peevish, silk-pyjamaed Arnold. The others would dribble in at various times later, usually after he had left for his beloved factory.

Alyss came in, though, soon after he had dug out his grapefruit. She looked bright and gave him the friendliest smile he had ever received inside that house from the family.

'Good morning,' he said.

'Good morning, suspect,' she retorted.

'So that's what makes you feel so pleased, huh?' He felt disappointed. That smile of Alyss's was good to receive.

She came away from the sideboard with her grapefruit. 'No.' She pushed back her dark hair with a quick little gesture, and now she wasn't smiling. 'I'm a reformed character, Russ. I've been getting around to it for weeks, starting to be kind to you instead of a beast.'

She spoke lightly, but suddenly Farran put down his spoon and stared at her. The kid was in earnest; more, her lip was trembling, almost as if she was about to cry. It astonished him — all his life he had known her as a pert, lippy, independent creature at war with the family almost as much as with himself.

She spoke again, nervously, jerkily, digging clumsily because she wasn't concentrating on the grapefruit.

'I guess I'm growing up, Russ. Guess I'm beginning to think for myself. Okay, lately I've been thinking what a lot of selfish beasts we are to you — all except mother, that is. And I've been as bad as the worst; I've been horrid to you all these years.'

She was crying now, staring down at the mauled yellow fruit in the crystal dish. 'I was brought up to believe you were everything horrid and detestable,

Russ. The others saw to that — Burt and Rita, Arnold and June especially. Lew's not bad, in spite of the way he cuts his hair. They never had a good word for the first Farran, and I was such a kid I thought it smart to be like the rest.'

Farran was touched. He went over and knelt by the girl, said soothingly, 'You don't need to say any more. It's nice to hear it, but it doesn't do you any good to say such things.'

She turned to face him, and her soft hands played with his coat collar, while she spoke earnestly — earnestly as the child she was. She wasn't crying now, though her round cheeks were wet with tears.

'I'm not against you any more, Russ. I've been thinking for quite a time, in fact, that you're the only brother worth having.'

'I am?' He was astonished, and yet inside there was a warm, melting, pleasurable feeling.

She nodded her head vigorously. She was smiling through drying tears. A nice smile, quite a nice kid. 'You're curt and you're grim, you do things quickly and efficiently, and — boy, have you a way of giving orders! But, Russ,' — she surveyed him tolerantly, head on one side — 'you're soft inside — nice, you know. I've just started to realise it. Russ, you've got a friend in the house now — me. After all these years!'

He got up, looking vaguely out of the window. 'Funny, I suppose that's how it's been all these years — the family ganged up against me. It's never occurred to me that it's been that way, me without a friend in the house. I suppose when you grow up to things you accept them without thinking. You tolerate in your home life things that would be impossible outside it.'

Alyss was watching him, the smile switched from her face suddenly.

'What are you looking at, Russ?'

'Oh, nothing.' Only an ape among the trees. Watching tirelessly, making sure he didn't try to skip the State. He came back to his breakfast.

'Why does everybody dislike me so?'

'Because from the first it was known

that you would inherit the Farran Empire. None of us have been able to forgive you for being born ahead of us — and scooping the pool. And you had a different mother. Things like that make a difference.' She grinned. 'It's your money we're after, Russ.'

'Maybe there won't be much soon.' He could joke about it, but he knew things were tough. He wouldn't come out of it a poor man, of course — he'd still have more millions than he could spend in a lifetime unless he let Burt help him go through it. But inevitably, losing control would cut down his holdings — and break his heart because building airplanes was more than a passion with him — it was his very life.

For some reason suddenly he remembered Karda, the Hungarian head of the Supersonic Experimental Section; for some reason remembered what he had once said to him.

A dry, stick of a man, Karda, yet brilliant. He had broken through one of Farran's enthusiasms to say, 'You're growing lop-sided, Mr. Farran. You spend all your time in the research departments. Now, your father gave his time to everything; your father ran every department, really.'

'I've got good men to run the other departments,' Farran had smiled. 'Me, I like research. I'm more useful here.'

'Oh, yes, you're useful.' Karda's eyes had twinkled. Russ Farran was more than useful, as everyone in the department knew. Russ Farran was the inspiration and the driving force behind most of their experiments.

'Still,' Karda had ended, 'the boss should keep an eye on everything. It's fatal to become a stranger to your workpeople.'

It was funny, suddenly remembering that long-forgotten conversation now. Farran sat back and considered. Was all the trouble with labour because he had grown apart from everything except the experimental side of the business? It was something worthy of deep thought at some later moment.

He remembered Uncle El. 'You got your story mussed up yesterday, Alyss,' he grinned. 'Nobody introduced any scab labour into the factory yesterday. But everyone thinks I intend to do so.'

'Well, that's queer,' began the girl, and then shut up because Darling McMee was coming into the room.

As they both rose Alyss whispered, 'That did it yesterday, you know, Russ. I mean, bringing Darling along. It brought me over to your side. It's like you to do nice things in a grumpy way.'

She flashed a quick smile at him. Farran softened inside. Tenderness and affection were something he had grown up without, and now that it came it completely disarmed him.

They went across to the girl. She was in a bad way, though striving hard to hold on to herself. She looked thinner, whiter even than yesterday. She smiled when she saw them, but it didn't touch that ache in her wider-than-natural blue eyes.

They led her to a chair, Alyss saying, 'What do you want for breakfast?' But she could only take coffee.

Farran made her talk, though. 'There's an inquest today. We both have to attend and give evidence. I'll take you along if you feel fit enough.'

'I'll make it.' She was like a ghost, sitting between them. But a little vigour came to her voice as she said, 'I've got to make it. I've got to do all I can to help them find Joe's murderer. He mustn't get away with this; the police must find him.'

Farran soothed the rising tide of hysterics. 'Sure, sure. We'll help the cops all we can. I'll bet they're right after that killer at this moment.'

And then he remembered the ape among the trees outside and a nasty feeling trickled down his spine. Maybe the police were so sure that he and the girl were complicit in the crime that they weren't looking further for the murderer. He thought, 'It was a bad break, bringing Darling to stay here with me. It won't look at all good.'

Then obstinately he decided it was what he would do again, even if he had known what it would lead to.

The inquest was an ordeal. The place was stiff with cameramen and reporters, because word had leaked out that he,

Russ Farran of the mighty Farran Empire, was involved in this killing. He gave his evidence abruptly, curtly, angrily; Darling McMee whispered her answers to the questions and swayed a few times as if almost at the end of her mental resources.

When they came out together Farran put his arm round her to support her.

A crowd was collected outside. Farran guessed that a lot would be from his factory, gawking at the boss.

And some of them started to hiss as they passed.

In the car Darling asked in bewilderment, 'Why did they hiss us?' But Farran didn't tell her the truth, that people were thinking things about them, as people always do in such circumstances.

Instead he said lightly, 'They're people on my payroll — when they're not out on strike. I reckon they kind of hate my guts.'

She looked at him, looked away as he started up. 'Why?' She was trying to work that one out. 'Why should people hate you? You don't look the kind to be hated.'

'You get yourself a couple of hundred million,' said Farran, 'and see how people react to you. Funny, money makes 'em hate you. They haven't a good word to say for you — only to your face in the hope of getting a chunk of those millions. But I'm used to it, used to being pointed out as a grinder of the poor, a flinty-hearted, uncaring taskmaster — a man concerned only in making more and more millions.'

'And you're not?'

'All I want is to build airplanes that fly,' he retorted, and then in a sudden passion he almost shouted, 'God in heaven, why won't they let me do it?'

Four more days and inevitably, because of chaotic conditions in the factory, he would be forced to resign from control of the firm, and inevitably that meant quitting the place completely — quitting it and leaving his life's work with little possibility of being able to resume it anywhere else.

It wasn't a happy thought. And suddenly he realised that until that meeting occurred he was virtually barred from his own factory. To go there, he thought wearily, could do no good and apparently would do only a lot of harm.

He let the speedometer needle drop as uncertainty took the weight off his pedal. How was he to spend the next few days?

He decided the best thing would be to get well away from L.A. and Farranville. Just keep out of the way and hope that things would turn up more favourable to him than past circumstances. He took the girl up the coast a hundred miles or so that day — and on the next couple of days, too.

That Sunday, Darling learned the meaning behind those hisses. She wasn't looking as bad now — still peaked, still white in spite of the long drives in the open car. But there was a greater firmness in her manner, that dazed, trancelike look had gone.

She grabbed Farran when he came down to breakfast that Sunday morning — and grabbed is the only word. There was colour in her cheeks, the colour that comes with high indignation. And her eyes were snapping as if she were completely outraged.

'Russ,' she exclaimed, 'why didn't you

tell me? What people are thinking about us?'

Farran saw Alyss lurking in the background. 'You've been talking,' he growled. 'I thought you were my friend.'

Alyss came across, her small round face pert with defiance. 'I thought she should know. While she doesn't it can make things bad for you. All this running around together. Russ, it doesn't look good.' Her voice was almost pleading. 'You're obstinate, but you've got to be discreet.'

'You mean, we should be avoiding each other?' Farran's lips twisted, looking at Darling's flushed, indignant face. He thought with approval that indignation made her look better than he had seen her look before.

Alyss said, 'I think you should be doing more than that. You don't seem to realise yourself what people are saying — and what people are saying, the police might be thinking.'

Farran looked out. The ape was among the trees again. 'Could be,' he agreed.

'So you should quit being a Rugged

Individualist and go see a lawyer. You should have done it days ago.'

'And stop seeing me!' The red colour burned in Darling's cheeks as she spoke.

Farran sat down. He was obstinate but he was intelligent. But he was also a fighter.

After a time he said, 'I should be doing more than that. I should be trying to find out who did it. That's the best way of clearing yourself — pin the crime where it belongs.' He got up. 'Darling, let's get down to that office and see what Joe was doing in the months he was here in L.A.'

'I thought we'd decided to keep clear of each other?'

Farran shrugged. 'We've left that a bit late, haven't we?' The damage seemed to have been done by now. He looked at her and felt that he didn't want to desert her now, anyway; found he wanted to stick by her in spite of public opinion and crudely expressed comment.

When they got to the office they found it so bare, the nursery rhyme wasn't in it.

Farran snapped his fingers. 'Why didn't we think of that. The police'll have impounded all the books in their search for clues.' He sat down, put his feet up on the desk. Darling sat on the edge of it. She hadn't liked coming to this room with its unpleasant associations in her memory, but she was game and hadn't said anything.

Farran said, 'Where do we begin? Not knowing what's in those books — '

'But we do — I do.' That was Darling, surprising him. 'You see, I kept Joe's books for him. I entered them up and filed his reports. And there wasn't that much for me to forget anything.'

'You weren't doing so well?'

'Starving. Well, getting near to it. That job up at your works was a life-saver.'

'So Uncle El came through with something, did he? Good for Uncle El.' For a minute he almost forgot to ask what the job was — he was a lousy detective even if he had millions. 'You didn't find many jobs coming your way when you first put your name on the door panel?'

'We had two in the two months before we got the Farran job. The first was a kitten that had got lost. We found it — a neighbour had taken it in. The second was a case we hadn't wanted to take — following an erring husband. We were relieved when we found he was a secret drinker and not a loose old man.'

'What was the job El Farran put on to you?' It was natural to include Darling in that word 'you', because he guessed that the girl had done the secretarial work around the office for her late husband.

'He wanted to trace a man. He'd had a name given of some industrial specialist — that's how he described him to Joe. He didn't know where he was except that he'd been at an address in Washington.'

'Washington?' For some reason Farran thought of that abortive call in his uncle's office the other day.

'Joe only came back the day before he — he died. He spent a week in Washington, so it made quite a big case for him. He was glad when he traced the man, because it meant we stood in good with Farrans — and we could do with standing in good with someone.'

Farran detached his mind from the minor problem of — what sort of an industrial specialist was his uncle trying to contact in Washington? The kind of specialist that needed a private detective to dig him out?

'This is sidetracking us,' he interrupted. 'We're not getting any nearer our murderer this way. What else is there I should know?'

She looked at him. Her blue eyes were very unhappy. She had a good, intelligent face, he thought, even though it was fine-drawn and showed the marks of suffering at the moment.

'There isn't a thing I can remember. We never had callers. We came to this coast to be away from unpleasant relatives, and we sure got away from everyone! Most of the time we sat and played checkers.'

Farran took his feet down. 'It's a crime without a clue. It wouldn't be good if the police were in the same boat, would it?' But he had a feeling they were up against a blank wall, too.

He crossed to the door. 'We'll call that ape in and get friendly and see what we can learn from a real detective. Who knows, maybe he'll co-operate.'

But he didn't feel very hopeful about anything worthwhile materialising from the conversation.

He looked down the corridor. There was no ape lurking modestly behind a palm tree. He went down into the reception hall, and that ape wasn't there, either. So he stood out on the sidewalk and glanced down towards the harbour. A cab was receding from him; he thought there was something big in the back that could have been the ape, but he couldn't be sure.

'Rugged Man seems to have taken a holiday,' he told the girl. 'He's nowhere around.'

Her face brightened. 'Perhaps they're not suspecting us any more?'

He said, 'Perhaps,' enthusiastically, but that was only to keep her in good spirits. More likely, he thought, there was another ape tailing them now, only they couldn't spot him.

He drove her back home after that, deliberately going round by the main gates of the Farran factory to do so. They were picketing the place, because picketing is a seven-day a week job and Sundays can bring in scab labour as well as any other day.

When they saw the familiar car come speeding along by the high wire fence, the strikers surged forward as if to see him better. They were a good distance away when he shot past the main gates — 'Out of stone's throw,' as Farran grimly said — but they heard the shouts of abuse and saw the clenched fists that waved threateningly at them as they passed.

'They don't like you much, Russ.' Her face was clouded. 'I'm sorry about that. I like you, and — and I guess I want other people to like you.'

'Not many people like me.'

'Do you give them a chance?'

He glanced at her, a smile coming to his face. 'Looks like Alyss has been talking.'

'Yes, we talk. She thinks a lot of you now, Russ, and she's dead against the rest of her family for behaving like heels towards you. She's going to persuade you to throw them out — all except her mother.'

'Alyss seems a changed gal,' he said

mockingly. 'She used to be a little devil towards me.' His eyes were intent on the mirror.

'You're not the kind to make friends easily, Russ — though we seem to get along.'

'Yes, we do.' It surprised him every time he thought of it. He put it down to pity, he was sorry for the girl. 'You came at a time when I was lonely, taken away from my job. And there's distraction in playing nursemaid when you have troubles of your own.'

Darling said, 'I'll never forget it, your kindness. You're really quite all right underneath, Russ.'

Farran squinted at that mirror again and said, 'I wonder if the guy tailing us in the car behind thinks that?'

His eyes narrowed. This was no taxi; it was a very ancient jalopy. Farran thought, 'Even my office boys wouldn't like to be seen in that.'

He slowed, hoping to see the driver's face. This must be the new tail, the substitute for the ape. But the light reflected on the windscreen and it just looked blank to him. So he accelerated suddenly, got round a bend and reversed quickly off the road.

They sat and waited.

The jalopy came steaming round, changed gear noisily and took the hill beyond.

Farran sat back in astonishment. 'Well, would you believe it?' he murmured.

For the driver of the jalopy was the big, saggy yawp who was always first for hamburgers at the strikers' mobile food bar.

5

There was another surprise when Farran got back to the house. A police car stood outside; in a reception room was the quick-smiling, agreeable lieutenant from Homicide. He had a sergeant and a patrolman in with him.

He started off, 'I'm sure you won't mind, Mr. Farran. We're wanting to check on some information that's come through to us.'

'Information?' Farran felt immediately that here was trouble, in spite of the friendly, deprecating manner of the police officer.

'Yes.' The question, when it came, shot out, and now there wasn't a smile to accompany it. 'You own a three-eight revolver, don't you? And you don't hold a licence for it.'

Farran cracked back, 'I don't have a licence and I don't have a gun. So come again.'

The lieutenant came. 'We've had a call — been told you've been seen practising with a three-eight in your grounds recently.'

'Someone's got a good imagination. Someone's invented that story, lieutenant, and by heck I'll roast 'em for it. Look, someone's trying to pin this crime on to me, don't you see?'

He felt Darling's hand on his arm, restraining him, and he realised that he was almost threatening the police lieutenant in his attitude and both the sergeant and the cop were closing in fast.

He patted the girl's hand reassuringly. 'Okay, I'm not going to bust him on the head or anything,' he growled. 'But this is getting me sore. Who's my friend?'

'Our tip-off? He didn't give a name. He said he was on the staff and would lose his job if he talked out of turn.'

'Anonymous!' Farran sneered. 'That doesn't help — God knows how many we have on the staff here!'

'If you're so sure the information is wrong — '

Farran fell into the trap. 'Go look for

yourself. If you find a gun anywhere in this house I'll be surprised. The Farrans never have gone in for gunnery.'

'Thanks. I'll take you up on that invitation.' The lieutenant rose quickly, very agreeable again. Farran realised he had wanted that permission. 'If you'll come with us we'll have a look at your room, Mr. Farran,' he said briskly, and before they quite knew what was happening everyone was climbing the stairs to Farran's secluded suite. Darling came, too, and Farran knew she was apprehensive because she was still clutching hold of his arm very tightly.

He wasn't bothered himself. He didn't have a gun, and he ascribed the anonymous phone call to some malicious troublemaker — probably not even on his staff at his house, but maybe among the strikers down at the gates. His thoughts flew to that scrub-faced yawp with the wise-cracking style. Maybe he knew something about it.

Then he thought, 'Maybe he's a cop, my new tail.'

And then he stopped guessing.

For the first thing they found when they started to hunt through the pockets of his coats hanging in the wardrobe was a three-eight revolver.

Farran's reaction was instantaneous. He took hold of Darling's shoulders, looked her straight in the eye and said, 'This is a plant. Someone put that gun there. Someone's trying to pin this murder on to me, Darling, but you mustn't think I did it.'

She looked at him, then she looked away. She was unhappy, troubled — uncertain. Completely out of her depth. He saw her put a trembling hand to her forehead and took compassion on her. He didn't ask her if she believed him, and instead released his tight grip on her shoulders.

The lieutenant was smiling though the smile never melted the ice crystals in his sharp, grey eyes. 'We'll take this for an examination, Mr. Farran,' he said briskly. 'Our ballistics' experts might find the barrel interesting.'

'You also hope they might find fingerprints on the butt.' Farran wasn't losing his head. He realised that a dangerous situation was developing for him. 'You're not going to arrest, me, are you, lieutenant?'

The officer looked shocked, as if that was a thought that couldn't enter his head. 'Good heavens, no.'

'Okay. Well, I'm going off to see my lawyer, Sunday or no Sunday.' He turned towards the door, spoke cynically. 'You don't need to worry. You've got a tail on me, I know.'

'I'm sorry about that — the tail,' said the lieutenant delicately. 'But sometimes such things are rather necessary, you know. Especially when valuable witnesses have the power to charter aircraft and — ' He shrugged.

'And skip out to cooler places, huh?' Farran said, suddenly, 'It's queer, finding that gun where you did. That ape of yours who's been tailing me, he went through my suite pretty thoroughly the first night be was put on to me. Didn't he?'

'That's a curious thing to say,' smiled the lieutenant.

'Curious my foot,' snapped Farran. 'I

guessed he'd do it, and I wasn't bothered if he did, anyway. That's why I brought him in for a drink — so's to let him see the place with a light on. Next morning I knew he'd been back because I'd been careful to bend collar stiffeners under the drawers. They'd all sprung out, next morning, proving someone had opened them.'

'You're a smart man,' smiled the lieutenant admiringly.

'Not smart — clear in my conscience. I knew he couldn't find anything to incriminate me.'

He hardly heard the murmur, it came so softly — 'But he did.'

'He did? What are you talking about?' He looked up quietly and saw Darling's blue eyes watching him. She wasn't at all sure of him now.

The lieutenant sighed. 'Forgive me for saying so, Mr. Farran, but we found some interesting correspondence, some letters all signed . . . Darling.'

The girl's hands flew to her throat in horror. 'But I've never written any to Russ — to Mr. Farran!'

'No, she didn't. Look, I'm going to see those letters. What's more we'll bring in that ape of yours to prove that there wasn't any three-eight gun in my apartment that night he gave it the once-over.'

'I think,' said the smiling lieutenant, 'you would be much better advised to consult your lawyer before taking any practical steps of that nature. We'll go now. Thank you for your hospitality.'

He even bowed towards Darling. He was a very well-brought up young man, even if he'd have hanged the lot as soon as smile on them.

That left Farran and the girl together. Farran looked helplessly towards her. 'What do we do now, Darling?' he asked, but his question really was, 'Do you believe what they believe? That I killed your husband?'

She half-turned towards him, but didn't look at him. He heard her say. 'This makes things so difficult to understand, Russ. I don't know what to think.' Then she lifted her eyes and met his. 'I can't really believe it . . . but that gun.'

Farran sighed heavily. 'Go on believing or not believing, Darling. It doesn't really matter just now. The people I have to convince are those cops. I'll drive right off to see my lawyer.'

'I think I'll move and — and go home. Maybe now I'll be able to stand it.'

He saw her throat work, the tears come to her eyes as she contemplated her loneliness. He was touched. 'I'll ask Alyss to keep you company. I think she'll do it. Come on, we'll go out and find her.'

Down the stairs Darling said, 'It might be true what you say.'

'That someone's trying to frame me?'

'Yes. After all, we know that I never wrote letters to you, don't we?'

'Yes.' He sighed again with relief. 'This business is so screwy I can forget important things like that. Of course we know it. Perhaps now you'll believe me — ' Then he stopped.

The hell, he couldn't force a girl to say yes or no to that sort of question. It wasn't necessary to know what she believed, anyway.

Alyss said 'Yes,' and got one of the

several chauffeurs around the place to drive them both into L.A. That left Farran free to attend to his own urgent affairs.

He got through to his lawyer's home, to be told that he was out but would be back within an hour. Farran said, looking at his watch, 'I'll be along at four, then. Yes, it's very urgent . . . Yes, this is Russell Farran speaking.'

It was three when he looked at his watch — a few minutes after, anyway — he remembered later. And it was exactly forty-five minutes later that they found a corpse in a blazing car on a track just off the Farranville road into L.A. But Farran wasn't to know about that till later.

Because he had nothing else to do he dialled his uncle at his office. Uncle El, the big shot tycoon, didn't stay home Sundays when there was a strike on.

Uncle El said, 'No, Russ, we haven't laid hands on that letter. I spoke to Lewen about it — '

'Who?'

'Lewen, the strike leader, the fellow that got the letter in the first place. He

107

says when he got it he tacked it up on a board outside his caravan, but after Art Andilla had seen it — '

'How come he came to see it?' Farran's voice was sharp; he was suspicious of everything now.

'He was coming in to the meeting in my office; Lewen shouted him across to see what he was putting up.'

'So Andilla didn't have a chance to see the signature closely.' Farran knew it had been a forgery, but he was wanting to know how things had been done.

'Pretty close. He has no doubts himself.'

'A good forgery can be made of any signature to pass even sharp scrutiny — but not a magnifying glass. I want to put a glass on to that letter.'

'That's what you said a few days ago.' Uncle El sighed fatly over the wire. 'I'm telling you what I've found out — that letter's gone. The men tore it down, and we can't get hold of it now.'

'That's mighty convenient.' Farran knew he was jeering, knew he must have sounded unpleasant, but nothing seemed to have effect on his uncle.

Uncle El said, 'It's what you could expect, a letter like that being mailed to strikers, threatening them.'

'The hell, as if anyone in their right senses would mail a letter like that to 'em!'

Then he went off to his lawyer and told him the whole story. His lawyer had been his father's. He wasn't a crook, but he used the law in a way that appalled some jurists sometimes. He was indeed a very successful man. And Farran respected him for his smartness but didn't have much time for him outside business.

His lawyer looked shrewdly at him through bushed up eyebrows. 'You're in a pretty tight spot, Mr. Farran,' he rapped. 'I've got an idea you don't understand yourself how tight it is.'

'Meaning?'

'That gun they found in your room — '

'The gun that someone planted there?'

His lawyer waved impatiently. 'Have it your way — the gun that was planted there, then. You know what's going to happen now, don't you?'

'They'll take that gun to a police laboratory and find it killed Joe McFee?'

'Sure. It couldn't be any other gun, of course. It would be a waste of time planting any other sort of gun on you, wouldn't it?'

'They won't find any fingerprints on it.'

'They don't need fingerprints when they find a gun in somebody's possession. So far as they're concerned, that's your gun. Well, Mr. Farran, I reckon within a couple of hours or so they'll be up to arrest you — and you don't get bail on a murder charge. Not like this, you don't.'

Farran shot out of his chair at that. His lawyer seemed to find satisfaction in having startled him. He said, 'I was right, you haven't realised the seriousness of your position. Mr. Farran, you're going to have one hell of a time keeping yourself out of a lethal chamber.'

Farran could only look at him and say, 'My God, how has all this happened?' A big shot — maybe a bit arrogant with it — one moment. Now being hustled out of his holdings and halfway towards an electric chair, too!

And how had it happened? He thought back. It was Lydia van Heuson who had started it all. He'd missed his turning just so that he wouldn't have to stop and pick her up and endure her efforts to revive a dead spark inside him. All that was over. She could find someone else — maybe her husbands . . .

He thought, 'Those letters!' Of course they'd be Lydia's. She'd been discreet because of her husband, had always ended, 'Your own darling.' Maybe she'd put 'darling' with a capital 'd', he couldn't remember; women went in for capitals.

Well, that was something now, but he didn't tell his lawyer what had just occurred to him. Those photostats wouldn't stand up when comparison was made with Darling's own handwriting, but they'd served their purpose — they'd helped to create this snowball of suspicion that had culminated now with the discovery of that planted revolver.

He started to drive back home — a mechanical decision to make — thinking, 'Who could have planted it? Who dislikes me so much they want to see me fry?'

And then he thought, 'Maybe the fellow doesn't dislike me. Doesn't know me. Maybe he's using me to divert suspicion from himself. I just happen to be here, a sitting target for things like this.'

Then he thought, 'Heck, maybe the cops are waiting back home to put the bracelets on me!' Or didn't they put bracelets on a millionaire's wrists?

It made him stop at the roadside to consider the situation. He didn't know what to do and he felt pretty helpless, but all the same he didn't panic. He lit a cigarette and tried to work things out.

He couldn't see daylight himself, so he reckoned the best thing now would be to buy the best private detective force in the country to start to trace the killer. The only thing was he'd left it a bit late.

From what the lawyer said, it looked like he'd sleep this night in the L.A. jail. He shuddered. It wasn't a pleasing prospect.

Straightaway he determined that he wouldn't go behind bars that day, not if he could help it. If he was going to be taken in he'd grab at least as many hours of freedom as he could.

He started to turn, thinking to get back to the beach and take out his sailing boat. He couldn't think of any place better, and he could sleep aboard tonight. In the end someone was sure to say Russ Farran had a boat out there, but even if it was for one night only it would be worth it.

Then he stopped again, remembering how conspicuous a car could look that had cost half a million dollars to build. If they were looking for him he'd never make the beach on the Farran Special.

He pulled off down a dirt track among small trees and bushes, then walked back on to the road. He would get a lift into L.A. and walk down to the beach. It seemed pretty safe.

He was still actually walking out into the highway when a car came waltzing round from Farranville. Farran's hand was up — then it came down.

An old jalopy pulled up alongside him. There was a lot of steam issuing from the battered radiator. Russ said politely, 'Did it have to be you?'

There was the big yawp behind the wheel, looking less shaven than usual, his attire even more slept in and weary-looking. He looked startled, seeing Farran there.

'You go too fast,' he complained. 'I tried to flag you, comin' out, but you went right by. This can gets hot an' I have to stop to let her cool.'

'You're a fine tail,' Farran scoffed, but he felt that there was something here that didn't quite gell. Why did a tail want to flag him . . . and why did a police tail use a useless can like this? He kept his mouth shut.

The yawp said, complainingly, 'I've been trying to do you a good turn, mister.'

So then Farran asked outright, 'You got anything to do with the police department, brother?'

The yawp gave a fair impression of a man being suddenly sick. 'I'm an honest man,' he said, aggrieved. 'I don't have nothin' to do with the cops.' He spat ruminatively on to the road, then said, 'Reckon I could say me an' the cops don't fraternize much at all, in fact.'

Farran sighed with relief. Maybe he could have his few precious hours of freedom on his boat, after all. He got in beside the yawp. 'We were heading for L.A., weren't we?'

'Where's your car?' The yawp experimented with the gear lever and found there was a position that gave movement to the vehicle. They shook off — that was how it appeared to the former Mustang fighter pilot.

'I'll tell you about that later,' said Farran easily. 'Just drop me somewhere in town near a station.' He thought that was dead cunning.

And then he demanded, 'Now, brother, tell me why you were trailing me.'

The yawp stopped kicking at a sticking clutch — or it might have been the footbrake — and coasted down a hill to cool the overheated radiator. He turned his scrubface towards Farran and said, 'Mister, you know that strike at your place ain't on the level?'

'It isn't? Brother, for that we'll stop at the next diner and I'll buy you a meal even if it kills me. What'll you have — hamburger or hotdog?'

'Hamburgers! I get sick of 'em. For six months of the year I live on 'em, them an' hotdogs. I get to hate the sight of strike food.'

He pulled in at an Italian joint in an orange grove. The bill said, 'Special — Chicken and French Fried.' The yawp said, 'If it's on you, mister, that's my dish. If it's up to me, I'll take coffee only.'

They got out, Farran saying, 'It's on me — and a lot more like it if you have anything to tell me. An awful lot more, brother.'

Even then he thought how curious it was that with the prospect of an electric chair grimly sitting before him, he could get concerned about the Farran strike. But that was how it was.

They sat up at the counter. The place seemed one favoured by truck drivers who were used to talking above the sound of threshing engines. It was pretty noisy, but that didn't worry Farran. They ordered. While it was coming up Farran decided to put a call through to Darling's apartment later. He thought he didn't want to have Darling and Alyss worrying, and he was pretty sure they would worry if he disappeared even for a few hours.

'Sure it's screwy,' the yawp was saying, grabbing a buttered roll as an appetiser. 'I know strikes — don't I know 'em better than any man in the country? An' my instinct says this is queer — screwy — not on the level.' He leaned forward, his jaws working, his narrowed eyes sharp and quick. 'They've been got at.'

'Who've been got at?'

'Lewen and the strike committee.'

'Look,' said Farran patiently, 'come clean with what you're saying. I don't get you one bit. What do you mean by 'Lewen's been got at'?'

The yawp hitched at his pants and then got back into his comfortable, confidential sprawl along the eats bar.

'I'm tellin' you. There's money being put out to Lewen and his pet boys — plenty money. They don't want to go back to work while they can earn big dough so easy, so that's why they keep on strike. Believe me, brother, a lot of those fellows would go back to work if they weren't afraid of the strike leaders.'

'Are you telling me that big money's being paid to foment trouble with my workpeople?'

'I can't make it plainer.' The yawp took off a bite, sprayed bread when he talked. Yet right then Russ Farran wouldn't have sat alongside anyone else.

Farran thought. Then spoke — bitterly. 'How do you know it isn't me? I get blamed for everything.'

'A fellow doesn't pay out big money just to give himself a headache. It's someone who doesn't like you, brother. Maybe you can think who.'

'Sure, sure, it's dead easy. Half of California seems to hate my guts.' He looked at the comfortable munching hobo alongside him. 'That goes for you, too, the way you shot your mouth off at me down at the gate that day.'

The yawp waved deprecatingly. 'Think nothing of it, brother. That was purely professional and it don't mean a thing.'

Farran opened his mouth and then closed it because a couple of chickens

118

came running up to them, along with a mass of French fried. He saw the yawp start to get around the food, ate a bit himself and then slid off to the phone. The yawp could elucidate later.

He found the number — got through to Alyss, though, not the owner of the apartment. And Alyss was crying. When she recognised his voice she wailed, 'Oh, Russ, you're in a mess, aren't you?'

He played cunning. 'What about, Alyss? Anything — happened?'

It sounded as though his lawyer had been right; the police had been around to arrest him.

There was a pause, as if she was trying to choose her words. Then: 'They've found him — the ape.'

'The ape?' It was his name but it took him a second to remember. 'My tail? What about the ape?'

'Don't you know?' He didn't like the way she said that. 'They found him in a blazing car just off the Farranville highway. He was dead, only . . . he hadn't been burnt to death as they wanted people to believe — '

'They?'

'The people who killed him. The people who beat him to death.' And then she said, queerly, 'The police think they know who killed him.'

Farran got it. It hit him in the stomach like a hard, physical blow.

'Don't tell me. It sticks out a mile, these days. If there's a corpse, pin it on to Russell Farran. Is that about it?'

'It is. We — we can't believe it.'

'Darling — does she believe it?' He spoke quickly, suddenly concerned to know the girl's opinion.

'She's trying not to, I think. She's — she's weeping for you now, also, Russ.'

He said, 'Bless you both for it,' and then suddenly cracked down the receiver and hurried over to the yawp.

He'd suddenly realised that all calls would be tapped to his home and Darling's apartment. They'd have traced that call a couple of minutes ago, and a radio car would be on its way to him right now.

6

He was still determined to have one more night of freedom — another night out of jail couldn't harm anyone or himself, he thought, and he even kidded himself that in that time he might even think of 'something'. He was very vague about what it could be.

He shoved his way through the burly, arguing truck drivers, all ferociously discussing someone's chances in a big fight or an even bigger ball game. The yawp was looking at Farran's plate with greedy eyes — his own was so clean they wouldn't need dishwashers if all customers were as thorough with their eating.

Farran snapped, 'C'mon, fellow. I need that jalopy of yours.'

The yawp came away from the counter with a handful of chicken from Farran's plate. They shoved out and got into the jalopy, which stood all alone as if even the commercial trucks wouldn't have anything to do with it.

'It's a good car,' wheezed the yawp, kicking and shoving like it was a mighty Wurlitzer. 'Six months of the year I get me a job some place so's to keep out the cold. The next six months we go from place to place.'

Farran still had the idea of sleeping out off Santa Monica beach that night. 'Just drop me off in town,' he repeated. 'And get back to what you were saying about this being a screwy strike.' As an afterthought he added, 'You can also tell me why you're doing this for your sworn enemy — the boss himself.'

As they pulled into the main stream of traffic, a police car with sirens demanding a clear road, zipped up to the diner, halted, and four cops went tumbling towards the wide open doors.

Farran thought, 'I should be safe, in a jalopy like this. They don't look for millionaires in old sardine cans.'

The yawp settled on a straight course and then looked at him. His eyes were grim, but Farran got an impression of

sardonic humour back of them. He was
beginning to like that bristly, blue-
chinned mug.

'No guy with as many millions as
you've got can be my enemy,' he said
cynically.

'But you gave me mouth like you hated
me?'

The yawp took his hands off the wheel
to wave deprecatingly. 'I told you, that
was professional. I eat their food, I gotta
earn it, see? I'm conscientious.'

Farran watched the road ahead. They
were wandering badly. 'I don't see,' he
retorted. 'And don't you talk with your
hands!' The car straightened. 'In other
words, you're coming to me with
information which you hope I'll buy?'

'That's it, brother. It's coming Fall.
Soon I'll have to hibernate, an' that
means workin' an' I don't like workin',
not if I can help it. Me, I'd like to winter
down Florida for a change, so's I could
watch the gee-gees.'

'If you can put me on to anything, I'll
grubstake you for more than a winter.'

He saw the big, weather-brown hands

tighten on the wheel. This was talk the big yawp had wanted to hear.

'That's talkin'. Okay, now I'll shoot my mouth. I got the feeling right from the start that that strike was somehow screwy. Lewen and his pals were fighting real hard to keep the men solidly out, an' — well, I figgered they were a mite too keen with their talk.' He looked through the cracked windscreen, trying to find words, then nearly gave it up. 'It just didn't ring.'

Farran said, 'I get you. But go on — you must have found something more concrete than an echo in someone's words.'

'I did. I got me a hundred bucks. Lewen shoved it into my fist the day I sassed you down at the gates. He said I was doin' fine an' for me to keep it up.'

'A hundred bucks? That's a lot to give to a picket.'

'Too much.'

'But you took it?'

'Sure. Then I hung around. It looked like it was payday. I kept seein' men drift into that caravan — they were the ones who do all the talking — an' because I was watchin' closely I saw there was money being handed round. I figgered there was a hundred dollars goin' out to every one of 'em.'

'And there were a lot?'

'Coupla dozen.'

'That makes big money.' There was a line of traffic ahead, held up by some obstruction. They rammed the rear car and that halted them. The driver of the other car got excited and did some shouting, but when he saw that battered jalopy and the equally battered driver he knew there was no future that way and he shut up in time . . .

'It's more money than a union can afford, an' it wasn't bein' given to everyone — just the talkers.'

They lurched forward, then had to stop again. Farran said,

'Things are beginning to fit.' He turned in his seat, his eyes blazing mad. 'Yeah, they're beginning to fit now. You've put me on to something, fellar, and I won't forget it.'

The yawp said, 'I won't let you,

brother.' They jerked forward again then stopped. Everyone was sounding their horns, but when the yawp tried to use his it wouldn't work.

Farran shouted above the din, 'It could be worth a lot to some people, to stop production on my planes. I always thought it was too bad, our record with labour. We got strikes when other manufacturers would have had a mild deputation. And when I try to show I just wanted to be friends with my workpeople — when I introduce a social security scheme — wham! Out they come again for the worst strike of the lot!'

They jerked forward another car length and then stopped. It began to puzzle the yawp, and he kept hanging out over the door to see what was happening up forward.

Farran said, 'It's a war contract we're working on. Could be there's international politics behind it.' He was trying to figure that angle out.

'Could be,' said the yawp. 'But it ain't, brother. They wouldn't have the money to lash out like this, an' it wouldn't pay them.'

'No, of course not. Then who will benefit by labour troubles at Farrans?'

The yawp fished something repulsive from the pocket he sat on. 'Find out who wrote that and you'll be gettin' somewhere.'

Farran unfolded the paper distastefully. It was stained and grubby on the outside, but the contents weren't difficult to decipher. It was a typewritten letter, with a bold signature at the foot.

Farran's eyes saw a few words and then his head came up in astonishment. 'This is the letter that was posted outside the strike leader's caravan. How did you get hold of it?'

He was looking at that signature. If he hadn't known he would have sworn that it was his own. He couldn't tell it from his normal signature, and only the fact that he knew he had never signed such a letter let him know the truth now — that it was a very clever forgery.

'I pulled it off when no one was lookin'. I reckon Lewen had intended to get that letter away himself, because he was mighty perturbed when it couldn't be found.'

Another jerk forward and then a halt. 'Why did you take it?'

'I figgered I might sell it to you,' the yawp told him coolly. 'The way things were, I got to feeling maybe that letter wasn't on the level. Is it?'

'It's not,' he said curtly. 'Don't think I ever wrote this damned thing. Thanks for it. It might save me my control on Farrans.'

'That's worth a lot, ain't it?' That yawp was no slouch with his brain. 'I'll sell it for ten grand, brother.'

'Ten grand?' Farran wasn't to be taken for a sucker. Ten grand for a letter; It was safe in his pocket, anyway. 'I'll give you five hundred for it.'

The yawp said, 'You'll give me ten grand — a cheque made out 'Pay Bearer' — now. An' if you think of arguin', just look what's ahead!'

Farran looked. It was a police barrier.

They were looking closely at the occupants of the cars going west, and Farran knew they were looking for him. They must have found the bird had flown from the diner back down the highway, and radioed for a roadblock to be set up.

He wondered if someone had spotted him climbing into the old jalopy. If so, he was sunk — if he wasn't sunk anyway.

When he looked at that grinning scrub face alongside his own he knew that the wise guy was wise to him.

'They want you, don't they? I got a word in between the horn play. Your name. What's it for, mister?'

Farran said, laconically, 'Murder.' Then he fumbled for the door catch. 'I'll get out. You don't want to be dragged into this.'

The yawp's big, hairy hand closed over his own. 'You don't get out yet, brother. You've got a letter worth ten grand. Make out that cheque first, before you do anything else.'

Farran pulled out a cheque book. He was fighting desperately now to think of some way out of this trap. The cheque book suggested it.

He said, softly, 'Maybe you could get me through this barrier, brother.'

The yawp looked at the cheque book and said, 'Maybe.'

'I could make this cheque out for twenty grand just as easy as ten, and with yesterday's date on it no one would ever know what it was for.' Ten grand didn't mean a thing to him, not like his freedom, anyway.

The yawp nodded, his eyes fixed calculatingly on the cars ahead. 'Try it,' be advised. When the cheque was torn out he looked at it, looked at Farran, and seemed satisfied. 'I reckon you're on the level with this,' he said, 'so I'll be on the level with you.' He started to pull the long seat cushion forward in the rear. 'You can get in there. They won't think to search this jalopy. It won't be comfortable, but you can get out in maybe five minutes.'

Farran climbed into the back and pulled the seat cushion on top of him. It stank and was stiflingly hot, but he knew he could bear it for five minutes. He heard the yawp say cheerfully, 'You'n me had better stick together, brother. We get on fine, don't we?'

Farran said coldly, 'One whole day together and I'd end up owning this jalopy and you'd have controlling interest in the Farran Empire.'

He heard the yawp say, 'Aw, the heck, I ain't got no ambition. Just give me twenty grand every coupla days an' I'll be satisfied.' And then the jalopy lurched forward. 'Sew your mouth now, brother,' the yawp advised. 'We're comin' up to 'em!'

Farran lay and sweated while they made two more jerky movements forward. Then he heard tough voices. 'Anyone in that car with you?'

'My dame,' cracked the yawp. 'Can't you see her or somep'n?'

The cop snarled, 'Fresh guy. Where are you from?'

'Farrans. I play picket these days there.'

'Farrans?' The cop was interested. 'You know the big boss there, then? Russell Farran?'

'Sure. Him an' me are like that.'

'Yeah.' The cop trailed dirt into the word. 'Maybe you've seen him, comin' down?'

'Sure.'

Farran stiffened, his lips pulling thin and hard. It was a mistake, maybe, to have signed that cheque just then. Better to have kept the signature off until the yawp had kept his bargain.

Then the yawp said, 'He was sittin' up at a diner with a rough-lookin' fellar could have been a truck driver.'

Farran sighed with relief. The yawp was square. Maybe he'd get more money out of him for this. The cop seemed satisfied and the jalopy exploded into movement again. A few minutes down the road and Farran heard the yawp yell, 'You can come out now, brother.'

Farran clambered back beside him. All he said about the incident was, 'Thanks, brother. You handled that cop well.'

They drove for a while in silence. Farran was doing a lot of thinking. When they came to Santa Ana he said, 'Keep left here.' He'd go through Long Beach and avoid L.A.

They chugged noisily along the coast road. Abruptly Farran said, 'Don't you want to know what it's all about?'

The yawp said, 'Sure. I c'n wait till you get round to it, though.'

He pulled up just then and bellowed to a kid with papers. They could see something exciting had happened because the papers were selling real fast. The kid couldn't even get over with a paper, so the yawp fell through the doorway and got himself one.

As he came back across the sidewalk the big, lumbering strike picket folded the paper across and Farran saw two big words smeared over the front — 'DETECTIVE KILLED.'

His pulse raced. That would be the ape. Maybe that paper would also print the name of Russell Farran in connection with the killing.

He froze in his seat, watching that scrub face as it bent to glance at the headlines. If this big slack guy knew that the heat was on him for a second crime — the murder of a police detective — he guessed he'd stop helping him right away. It amounted to suicide, helping the suspected murderer of a cop.

Then he relaxed. The yawp took in the headline only, then climbed back into the car. 'That c'n wait till later,' he grunted. They rattled off again. 'Where did you say, mister?'

Farran made up his mind. He was determined to have one more precious night of freedom before walking in on the police. He thought, 'If I let this yawp out of my sight and he sees what's in that paper, he'll go put the cops on my track.'

So he said, 'Doing anything tonight?'

The yawp breathed on his nails and went through the motions of polishing them. 'Maybe I'll change an' go some place classy,' he cracked in a high-toned voice.

'Okay, how about sleeping aboard my boat for the night? She's small — five metres — but there are two berths and plenty of canned food. I'd like more talk with you.'

'Food?' He was interested. 'You talked me into it. Say where.'

They left the car in a public park near to the beach. Farran's dinghy was at the clubhouse, and he wasn't showing his face up there, so he put someone's dinghy into the water without asking for permission and took the yawp across in that.

Farran sighed with relief when he

pulled alongside his boat and no one popped out of the cabin to challenge him. It was likely no one would think of coming out here for at least a day. Maybe they wouldn't find his car for quite sometime and would be looking all over California for it — that and watching the airports.

It was coming cool now and they ducked into the tiny cabin. The yawp's first job was to open a locker and appraise the food within. It seemed to satisfy him.

They both stretched out on the bunks. For the first time in hours Farran felt he could relax; only then did he realise the strain that had been upon him all that afternoon.

He lay with his eyes half-closed, lulled by the gentle rocking of the boat into something very near to slumber. Reflecting light from the quick little waves wove a bright pattern on the ceiling.

He thought, 'This is better than lying in a cell.' Because he knew that if he hadn't run for it that's where he'd be now. They didn't give bail for murder charges, his lawyer had said.

Drowsily he thought, 'Maybe I should keep under cover as long as I can. They no longer believe that a man is any guiltier if he tries to duck out of trouble. When they go for me, it'll have to be real evidence they present.' Yeah, his highly paid attorneys would see to that . . . being a millionaire had some advantages.

With startling abruptness he jerked out of the calm into which the rhythmic rocking had sent him.

For the yawp was fumbling around for the paper he had bought. Farran thought frantically. 'I've got to keep him from reading that.' You couldn't expect a yawp to sit quiet knowing he was being sought by the police for the murder of a detective.

'Got anything else to tell me? About that queer strike?'

The yawp stopped shaking the paper out looked up at the dancing light on the ceiling again and said, 'Yeah, yeah. There was somep'n else. Somep'n else that don't fit.'

The hand relaxed about the paper, then the yawp rolled to face his companion.

Farran saw the heavy, weather-beaten face screw up under pressure of intensive thought, heard the dry bristles scrape as he scratched his frowsy chin with black-edged nails.

The fellow was a tramp, but Farran would put up with him so long as he didn't read that paper. Maybe if he could stall for an hour or two it would be too dark to read in comfort.

'You tell me,' he invited, to keep the fellow going.

The yawp did. And his words nearly brought Farran tumbling off his bunk.

'Did you know the Detroit Chopper Boys was interested in your strike?'

7

Farran said; 'What?' And then he said it again only this time even louder. He jerked up on his bunk, cracking his head against the open port glass. It made him wince but he ignored the pain after that.

'The Detroit Choppers? What're you talking about?'

He couldn't believe it. He was going back to that case a couple of years ago that had filled the newspaper columns of all America.

'They're here,' he heard the yawp growl emphatically. 'Some of 'em, with a lot of new Choppers. I know 'em, I tell you. Don't I know more about strikes than any man in America?'

Farran swung into a sitting position. His mind refused to see clearly the implications behind the strike picket's words. The Choppers . . . that was the case Joe McMee had buttoned lip so well. Joe McMee . . .

He said, 'Let's get this straight. The Choppers were stuck into jail after that Detroit business. Some of 'em got the chair.'

'An' some got away.' The yawp swung into a sitting position, too, his big form spreading where the edge of the bunk caught under him. He began to smooth that paper across his knees, and Farran didn't even take any notice of him then.

'Yeah, some got away. There was a lot of Choppers, a whole lot. An' them that ducked an' got away is mostly eatin' strike food outside Farrans right now. How do I know? Wasn't I there, in Detroit?' Then he looked cunning. 'But I knew them before that. They did other jobs before the F.B.I. got 'em at Detroit.'

Farran was remembering. Queer how quickly you can forget, too.

A sensation had burst upon America when some directors of a big automobile works in Detroit were brought before court to face serious charges. The evidence unfolded proved a revelation to most people.

It was revealed that there was a gang of

industrial saboteurs available for hire either to employers or to striking unions. By the sound of it, they'd been used a lot, too.

In Detroit they had been used to get some strikers in bad with an arbitration board set up by the Government. The auto works had been idle for several weeks because of a pay dispute, and a bitter, ugly situation had developed between strikers and management.

Some die-hard directors had decided to weaken the strikers' case before the arbiters, and they had hired out the Chopper Boys to do it for them. Only they weren't called the Chopper Boys until after that Detroit affair, of course.

They smuggled in twenty or thirty Choppers into the works one night, and told them to wreck part of a long assembly line. It was due for demolition soon, anyway, so the bosses weren't losing much by the wrecking. They figured, though, that the action would be ascribed to hotheaded strikers and it would prejudice their case before the board. Which is how they wanted it.

But things didn't quite go right this time. The Choppers were swinging sledgehammers and long axes when they were surprised by some executive workers who hadn't been expected in the works that night.

Two of the executives had died in the brawl that followed. At the inquest it was revealed that both had died from axe wounds, and from that moment the gang received the label of 'Choppers.'

The directors were sent down for long sentences, and then the heat was turned on for the Choppers. One by one they were picked up and made to stand trial. Three were sentenced to death, four more to life. The rest wouldn't get out of jail for a long, long time.

And Joe McMee had been the relentless bloodhound who had followed the Choppers all over America and brought them to book, though he'd been half-killed in the process himself.

Now this hobo was telling him that the Choppers were here — or what was left of them — participating in this strike. His immediate thought was that the workers had hired them to perform their skullduggery, but then it didn't seem to fit with what he knew of his people.

'What're they here for? Who'll benefit by having Choppers in on this strike?' he demanded.

The yawp was sitting very silent, watching him under rugged eyebrows, his big hands had the paper tight-stretched over his knees.

'What's back of it all?' Farran demanded. 'You got bright ideas, you tell me.'

But what he was trying to connect was some relation between the Chopper boys at his gate and Joe McMee's death. He was thinking. 'If they saw Joe, if they thought he was still tailing them . . . '

It was a theory. It was a whole lot better theory, anyway, than to think that he, Russ Farran, should be nailed for the job.

He swung his legs in quick, nervous movements. His heart was beating fast, shoving hot blood to circulate through every part of him. It made him feel strong, made him feel he wanted to get into some action. For he felt that he was getting down to things at last.

'Maybe it's a good thing not to get stuck away in a police cell,' he was thinking. 'If I'd just let 'em take me I'd never have learned what I know now. Maybe I won't just surrender tamely tomorrow.'

Then he thought, 'I must tell Darling about this. When she knows about the Chopper Boys she'll stop thinking I used that gun.' And his heart started to bump like the old jalopy engine, because he didn't want Darling McMee to go on thinking like that of him.

He came out of his trance. There was something queer about the way the yawp was staring at him.

He demanded, 'You ill?'

The yawp's blue chin dropped as he started in to speak. He spoke very deliberately, very toughly. 'I look soft but I ain't soft, mister. I know every dirty trick they ever thought up outside a wrestlin' ring.'

'Meaning?'

'I'm leavin' you, that's what I mean. An' if you try'n stop me, so help me I'll break your neck!'

He was watching Farran's hands now, as if expecting to see them dive somewhere and maybe come up with a gun. He was a very alert hobo at that moment.

Farran's eyes dropped to the newspaper. He sobered, understanding. 'You've been reading the paper. What's it say?'

'It doesn't say you killed a detective called Charlie Mulhoney. They never say that before a trial. But it leaves no doubt the cops think you did it. He got burned, back near your house, only he was dead before he started cookin' an' the way he died it couldn't have been suicide.'

The yawp slid off the bunk and went backwards up the few steps on to the deck. Farran just looked at him and couldn't think of a thing to say.

The yawp said, 'Brother, you're hot. I ain't gonna be found with you, because the cops might get to thinking I did things to that detective, too.' He sighed and pulled out the cheque. It cost him an effort. 'Reckon I've got to pass this up, too. They'd think things, if I presented this.'

Farran waved it back. Money didn't have much meaning in his position. 'Keep it. You never know, things might settle out.' Then he rapped, 'Are you going to tell the cops where I am?'

The guy hadn't thought so far. 'Guess I don't know what to do. All I know is, I ain't stayin' with you.'

Farran said, urgently, 'I don't want you to talk. Look you've told me a lot that's interesting. It helps — you don't know how it helps. Things are beginning to add up, though I don't know yet what the final total is going to be.'

He licked his lips, but his eyes never left that big yawp framed in the hatch opening.

'Look, brother, I want my freedom. I've got a feeling I can use it to clear myself. I tell you, you've told me a lot that's helpful. Maybe I'll be able to find that bit more that'll clear me altogether.'

And then he snapped his fingers, staring into the disbelieving scrub face that watched him so narrowly.

'The heck, you're the one man that knows I didn't kill Mulhoney.' He thought back. 'The only time I wasn't with people today was between three and four o'clock. That's the time I was in my room at the house.'

The yawp said, 'That's the time they found the blazing car — four o'clock.'

Farran guessed it would be. It had to be like that, if he was to be linked with the crime. Everything always looked its blackest these days when Russ Farran did anything or was even supposed to have done anything.

Farran said, 'All right, then you know I didn't kill that cop. You said yourself you were hanging around the gateway, hoping to catch me when I came out. Only, when I came out I came so quickly you never saw me. What time was that?'

'Just before four.'

'And you tailed me right out of the district. Look, if they found that poor 'tec cooking at four o'clock, he must have been killed sometime before. And you say yourself it wasn't far short of four when I left the house, so you know I couldn't have done it.'

'Maybe you went out another way and

did for him, then came back.'

Farran said, 'Maybe. Only there isn't another way.'

'Over a wall?'

'All right, over a wall. But do you think that's credible?' He shoved his face forward toughly.

'A jury could believe it.' The guy looked at him. Then he said, 'Maybe this is another frame up, I don't know. All I know is, I ain't gonna be found in your company, brother. I'm goin'.'

'But you'll keep your mouth shut?'

'I'll keep it shut.' The yawp stroked the pocket where the cheque lay. 'An' I hope to God you clear yourself, because if you don't this li'l fortune won't be worth a dime to me. So long, brother.'

He stepped into the dinghy. Farran came out on deck. His first action was to look round quickly, but the nearest boats were a good distance off and no one was looking his way that he could see.

The yawp hesitated. 'How are you gonna get ashore?'

Farran told him — 'I'll swim. I often do. Lots of people do hereabouts, so it

147

won't attract attention.'

The yawp shoved off. He looked very big in that boat; his heavy arms made the oars seem rather small and child-like. He said, 'Good luck.' Then paused. Farran realised that he meant well by him.

'You know what you should do? Knock the shine out of them eyes. You're too much the bright-eyed boy, an' people'll be lookin' for bright-eyed boys. Eyes attract attention. Make 'em bleary an' no one'll recognise you — not with a scrub like mine, anyway. An' a towel round the middle makes your figure all different.' He was helping a lot. 'You got old clothes?'

Farran nodded. 'Jeans. Thanks a lot fellar. That advice is appreciated. Maybe I'll be seeing you.' Then the yawp pulled away.

A couple of hours later Farran had made two decisions.

'The heck, I'm not giving myself up — ever,' he told himself. 'If they want me, they must come an' take me.' He felt that while be was in circulation he had a chance of remaining alive for a long time.

But not if they took him up and put him where he couldn't follow up on what the yawp had told him.

The second decision — where to hide. And he'd thought out a good hiding place. He thought, in fact, he'd hit on the safest hideout for Russ Farran in all America.

He'd go join the pickets right at his own gateway. That was the last place anyone would think of in the search for Russ Farran, wanted on two murder charges.

Those two decisions in mind, he did a few chores, such as throwing his suit overboard so as to confuse them if it were picked up, then he went to bed and slept very well for a man carrying his weight of trouble.

He swam ashore at crack of dawn, holding his bundle of clothes one-handed out of reach of the water. Back along the beach he made a careful toilet. It consisted, as much as anything, of rubbing dirt into his skin, not only on his face but also his forearms. And when he had finished he was pretty sure no one was going to think of the millionaire Russ Farran when they looked at him.

He was wearing an old shirt and jeans that he used when sailing, deck shoes that weren't at all the sort you'd expect to find on a wealthy man's yacht. He'd taken the yawp's advice and tied a towel round his middle; it wasn't comfortable but he felt that it destroyed the familiarity of his normal slim-waisted appearance. And the previous night he had chopped his hair a lot with scissors before a mirror and the result made him look rough and scrub-headed. That and the dirt on his face made a pretty effective disguise.

He gave a lot of thought to making his eyes bleary, as the yawp bad suggested, but it beat him. He couldn't think how it could be done. He felt it was important, getting the shine out of his eyes; he knew himself how distinctive, a man's eyes were to his appearance. But he couldn't think of a way just then, so he caught a train out to Farranville and risked it.

The lot in front of the big Farran gates was very crowded that morning. Plainly things were coming to a head, and the strikers were in force to witness events.

Farran went in among them with his body tensed, expecting for certain he would be recognised. But no one looked twice at him, and within seconds he had a curious feeling of exhilaration because he could walk among the men who hated him and be undetected.

He found it illuminating, moving from bunch to bunch of strikers. They always seemed so solid, so one-minded, strikers; as the boss, looking at them, meeting and arguing with them, you never thought of them being divided among themselves, of indulging in back-biting, petty jealousies, and scheming to get more attention to their own point of view.

Farran, walking among them, learned a lot that morning. There seemed to be a rising tide of opinion against the strike. Men growled that they'd had enough; they had kids at home and they couldn't go on like this. They said, 'It don't seem so bad after all, that social security scheme. God in heaven, what made us jump out so quick?'

But there were other men among them

— the out-and-outers who keep strikes going out of sheer cussedness . . . and men with the hundred-dollar look.

That's how Farran got to think of them as the morning went by. In time he came to recognise their breed — quick-talking, fast-thinking, ready to interfere and turn a topic or squash with biting sarcasm any conversation that seemed against the strike. They were, seemingly, there on the fringe of every little crowd — the backbone, the spirit and the very reason for the strike.

And Farran thought, 'They work hard for their hundred-dollar bonuses. They do their job well.'

He looked around, too, for signs of the Chopper Boys, but if they were there he couldn't recognise them.

Then a whisper came round that there was to be a big meeting at the Farran works that afternoon. The vine said there were to be changes in the management — Russ Farran would be thrown out. It seemed to make everybody cheerful, that thought, Farran noticed sourly.

He heard somebody say, 'He's the

cause of all the trouble. The things he's done against labour since I've known him! I guess he hates the guts of the workers, the cunning schemes he's cooked up. Now, this last one — '

'I don't see it's so bad now,' spoke up an old boy, some sort of assembly hand, Farran thought. 'In fact, it looks kinda good.'

'Yeah,' jeered the other man. 'It looks kinda good, but it ain't — dope! Nothin's good that's got the signature of Russ Farran to it. Now, if that scheme had been put up by some other guy, some guy we knew was on the level — '

A lot of men said, 'Yeah, yeah,' quickly. 'It's that Farran fellar. We don't trust him, an' we don't want no truck with him.'

'Sure,' said the first speaker. 'That's the way it is. You c'n see the kind of guy he is, writin' a threat like he did. A guy that can bring in scab labour just asks for trouble.'

Farran thought, 'They're so pumped up with poison against the name of Russ Farran, they wouldn't take a million if I gave it them.' That was why they had strikes, why this one wouldn't end.

Because of distrust of himself.

He was looking at the agitator and thinking he'd be a hundred-dollar boy, when they began to talk about the murders.

It became apparent there wasn't a man there who didn't believe implicitly that he had killed Joe McMee for love of his wife, and then battered in the head of the detective who was keeping him under observation.

When he heard this conversation he found he had to walk away. You can't hear such things about yourself without wanting to jump forward and hit somebody or at least shout out they're wrong, they don't know what they're talking about.

But either action would have been suicide, so he walked away whenever that subject came up.

He hadn't seen the big yawp that morning, but as soon as he saw the mobile diner come rolling into the park he guessed he'd be able to get a line on the fellow.

He did. That bulging gut at the head of

the queue could only belong to the loudmouth himself.

He came away with a cup of coffee in one hand, and a whole meal in his other fist. And he was talking — that man never stopped talking. Only as he went by Farran realised that the yawp's tune had changed. He was arguing they should go back; they were being made suckers over this strike.

Farran felt grateful to the big hobo for that. He recognized that in his queer way the yawp had taken a liking to him — or maybe he was sympathetic — and this was his attempt at helping him. Though even the yawp should have realised by now that it was too late; there wasn't much that could help Russ Farran.

He got into the queue himself, and in time came away with a meal. It raised his spirits to think how he was putting one across his sworn enemies.

He thought, 'Heck, it's too easy. Anyone could do it. Just get into a queue and if you're dressed for the part . . . '

His thoughts trailed away. He was looking at the yawp, thinking. He was thinking, 'Yeah, maybe that's it. Maybe that's the explanation!' For on looking back there was a lot that the yawp had said that hadn't seemed to fit, somehow.

He went and sat on the running board of an old truck that was used by the strikers to run up chairs and beds for the men at night. Some minutes later, when he was brooding into his coffee, a shadow fell over him. He looked up, then let his eyes come down again.

The yawp was standing over him, wiping his big wet mouth with the back of his hand. He moved and sat down beside Farran, and the millionaire felt the whole truck sag as the weight came down on the running board. He didn't look up, but he knew he had been recognised. He wondered what the yawp would do now.

He heard that familiar growl, like a bucketful of wet gravel, he thought.

'You ought to have done as I said. Strikers out in the sun don't have pretty eyes like yours. The rest of you's all right.'

Farran said, 'I couldn't figure out how to blear my eyes.'

At which the yawp came back with the word — 'Tobacco. Rub it in your eye corners. It'll hurt like hell, but you'll be bloodshot in no time.'

Farran swallowed quickly and nearly choked.

The yawp never looked at him, but kept rubbing his big slack mouth and talking behind the hand. 'You oughta get away from here. The town's crazy with cops lookin' for you.'

Farran looked into his cup and said, 'I'm safe here. I'm not moving, anyway, because I figure I might learn something useful.'

'Come again?'

'What you don't realise is that the G-man who tracked down the Chopper Boys was Joe McMee.'

'Him that got killed?' The yawp made repairs to his shoelaces.

'Him that got killed.' Farran felt satisfied suddenly; he began to feel that the yawp wasn't altogether disbelieving him, and that was something.

'Could be it was a Chopper killed him?'

'Could be.' Then Farran asked, 'What're

157

the Choppers doing in the Farran strike, anyway?'

'Beats me. They've done nothing so far 'cept hang around among the men here. Maybe they're bein' held back until they're really needed.'

'How?'

The yawp shrugged. 'Maybe if some-one thinks you're not licked right out, maybe then they'll come into the picture. Though don't ask me how.'

Farran began to see real daylight from that moment. He murmured, 'Leave me; I've got things to think out. Maybe we'd better not be seen too much together. I'll find you if I want you.'

The big lug got to his feet, and the truck wheezed a whole chorus of thanks. 'How'll you find me among all these uglies?'

'I know one place you'll always be,' Farran said cryptically, and when he understood the yawp looked indignant. Farran also said, 'I'm getting wise to you, too, brother. Things that didn't add up before. How long've you been on the Farran payroll?'

'Never,' said the yawp promptly.

'I guessed as much. What're you doing picketing the gate and shouting abuse at the boss, then?'

There was a grin on that blue-chinned mug. 'Me,' he said proudly, 'I'm the only professional picket in all the Yew Ess Ay. I collect strikes like some people collect stamps an' old furniture. You can't mention a big strike in the last ten years that hasn't seen me shoutin' things at the boss. Leastways,' he admitted, 'not during the warm months, when sleeping out ain't no hardship.'

'It's a queer hobby.'

'Man,' said that yawp, 'it's a fine one. There's excitement all the time, plenty of grub, lots of people all around to argue with — and you don't have to work.' He was very sympathetic about the last advantage.

'You don't like work?'

The yawp looked withering. 'Am I crazy? Who'd work if he didn't have to? I don't live high but, brother, it suits me!'

Farran let out a sigh. 'Maybe you're no worse off than people who live a whole lot higher.' Like himself, for instance. Living high hadn't made life all that easy for him.

He watched the big tramp amble off to join a high-powered argument around the strike leader's caravan, then he crawled under the shade of the old truck's tailboard and started to think up a short cut out of the jam he was in.

He didn't, of course. Couldn't. It wasn't the sort of mess a man could brilliantly think himself out of. In fact in two hours he didn't think up anything good that looked like helping him, though he'd begun to see the picture a whole lot clearer now.

Then he saw a big car approach the gates. The pickets let it pass. It occurred to Farran that the car looked like Art Andilla's, the bank nominee's, and then he suddenly remembered.

'The hell, it's Monday!' Monday, and that fateful meeting when his position with the company was to be discussed by shareholders and directors alike. Thinking of the headlines he was making, he didn't think anyone was going to ask him to stay on the board . . . and Andilla was in a position to make him resign.

Andilla's car was the beginning of quite a procession. Within the next twenty minutes they rolled up by the dozen — it was evident that the shareholders were arriving in force to discuss the company's situation.

He lay on his side and watched them go in. There was quite a watch on that gate. First the pickets took a glim at the car-occupants, then the gate police. And then a squad of Los Angeles cops took over and had a close look at them.

Farran knew they were looking, perhaps not very hopefully, for him to turn up at this meeting. He didn't think he was likely to attend. It would have to go its way without him. That could mean only one thing — he'd be forced from his position as head of Farrans. It made him writhe to think of it. He knew now he was being outsmarted, was being jockeyed out of the way, but realisation had come too late . . .

He got up suddenly and went in search of the yawp. It took him a long time to find the lug, and even longer to get him out of an argument that was cousin to an Irish brawl. But in the end that blue jowl turned his way, the eyes recognised him, and when he walked back to the old truck the hobo shambled up after him.

Farran said, 'I wonder if you've got the guts?'

'Me? For what?' — suspiciously.

'To attend an extraordinary company meeting as my nominee.'

The yawp fingered the bristles on his chin and said, vaguely, 'Yeah, sure . . . What's that?'

Farran explained. 'They're all sitting around inside that place just carving me into little strips. I can't attend the meeting, and that means they can do as they like with me. But look, you could go and talk to them. Maybe you could convince them that these labour troubles are all inspired to hurt me.' He paused. 'That's your idea as well, isn't it?'

The yawp spat into the dust. Farran took it to be an affirmative. That helped.

'Okay, that's all I ask — you tell 'em what you really believe.' He took the grubby letter from his pocket. 'Look, I'll give this back to you. Read it out to 'em, let 'em see it. Then give it to the police and ask 'em to check that the signature's a clever forgery and see if there's any fingerprints. Maybe they might even trace the machine that typed the note.'

'Betcha if they do I know whose machine it'll turn out to be.'

'Whose?'

'Yours.'

'If they do, then I'll know who's fathering all these troubles on to me,' Farran said grimly. He took out his pen and started to write on the leaf of a diary. It authorised the bearer to act at the meeting in place of Russell Farran 'unavoidably detained.'

Farran said, 'You're not scared?'

The yawp looked disgusted. 'Me scared of addressin' a meetin'?' He didn't have nerves, that professional picket.

Farran said, 'I've put Saturday's date to it. Keep saying you haven't seen me since and they can't do a thing to you. Now what's your name? That's to go on the letter, of course.'

Funny, he hadn't realised it before, but he'd never heard the fellow's name. The yawp looked at hom queerly, that lurking grin in the narrowed eyes. He said, slowly, 'Write down 'The bearer's name is Death'.'

'Death?'

'Sure, that's my name — Jim Death. It used to be 'de'Ath,' but the family democratised it when they landed in America.' He found his favourite spot in the dust and spat again into it. 'Me, I don't like the name. I get most people to call me Mac. But you had to have it, I guess.'

Farran said, 'It'll shake 'em. So what? I want you to shake 'em from the word go.'

The big yawp was scrubbing through his blue bristles, thinking hard and shooting quick little glances at Farran. 'It's a tough assignment,' he growled. Then he took out yesterday's cheque and looked at it. 'You made a mistake in writin' this up,' he complained.

Farran looked at it. It seemed all right and he said so. The yawp yawped, 'The heck, you said thirty thousand, didn't you?'

Farran caught on and altered the cheque, initialling the alteration to Jim Death's satisfaction. He thought, 'Ten thousand's nothing if this works!' Because he was beginning to see how the problem might be made to solve itself.

The yawp started off. Farran called him back. 'Look,' be said, 'if you see my sister, Alyss Farran, inside give her a message from me, will you? She should be there. She'll maybe come and speak to you,'

'You forgot the message.'

'Tell her to be in Lacey's at six.'

'Lacey's bar?' The yawp wouldn't miss a place like that. 'What're you goin' to do? Where are you goin' tonight?'

'I'll be a good picket and stay the night here,' Farran grinned. 'It's still the safest place for me.'

'I'll come back, too,' growled the yawp. 'You keep outa my way, though. I reckon the cops'll be watching me after I show up with this letter.' He looked pensive. 'Maybe it's not worth thirty thousand dollars.'

Farran warned, 'The men mightn't like

you, brother, standing up there and saying nice things about me. They'll get to know soon, you can bet.'

The yawp said, 'The men? Yeah, I c'n manage the men, brother!' And he went across to his car.

He showed cunning, that big lug. He drove out the far way from the park, came on to the road half a mile down, and then rode back to the gates.

That old jalopy caused more stir than a stick in an ant heap. Farran, watching from a distance, saw everyone go into a huddle at once, pickets, gate police and the cops. They kept looking at the paper the yawp held in his dirty great paw, kept firing questions at him — the cops, anyway — and the yawp just sat there and yawped back at them.

He could hold his own with his tongue anywhere. He was allowed in without overlong delay, but Farran had an idea he mightn't get out of the place so easily.

He went back to the shade of the tailboard, closed his eyes and tried to imagine the scene when that big tramp climbed on to the platform and insisted on talking to those slick, city shareholders and directors. He had a feeling that the fellow would handle that part pretty well, too.

When the meeting broke up, and streams of cars came through the big gates, he kept watch for the old jalopy but it wasn't in a hurry to come through. Farran thought the cops would have the yawp by now and would be grilling him. The fellow was going to earn his money from now on, but he guessed he was the kind to survive.

It never occurred to him to think that Jim Death might weaken and split on him. It was funny, the implicit confidence he had in that hobo now — and it wasn't because of the money the fellow could get out of him.

It wasn't far from six now, so he took a chance and stood out in the road and thumbed a lift from a shareholder's car going into Farranville. That shareholder bellyached all the way into town of the money he was losing through this strike, and for Pete's sake couldn't the men get any sense into 'em?

Farran said, 'Sure, but that guy Farran — '

'Farran?' snapped the shareholder. 'Look, you fellows might get taken in easy, but not people like ourselves, shareholders in the company. You don't think we swallow this rot about Farran causing this trouble, do you?'

'You don't?' exclaimed Farran.

'The heck, no! It's standing out a mile — someone's tryin' to get a load of dirt on his name. These labour troubles are being cunningly fostered by someone who wants to do him harm.'

'But you haven't fallen for it?' Farran's heart was singing. That grating, arrogant voice was nicer to him then than the Andrews Sisters'.

'No, sir! A fellow came today an' showed us the evidence.' He paused to reflect. 'He was a queer fellow to have as nominee at a shareholders' meeting, but he could talk — '

'Sure,' nodded Farran, 'he yawps.'

'The moment he handed that letter over to the police we knew he wasn't kidding about it being a forgery. He daren't stick his neck out over that. And if it was a forgery, then it put Farran right in the clear.' He chuntered for a while longer, then said, 'But what do *you* know about the letter?' and looked disgusted at having wasted so much breath on a striker.

Farran said, 'So they didn't do anything about Farran?'

'Nope.' He couldn't help it; that fellow liked to have an audience. Maybe he was kept under by his wife at home. 'One of the directors stood up and made a powerful speech, saying he'd suspected for a long time there'd been a whispering campaign deliberately fostered to blacken Farran's name among you men. He said for to leave things as they were on the board and tell the men what was happening. He sure spoke up in Farran's favour.'

Farran, bewildered, was thinking, 'Holy gee, they're all coming round to love me now! That Death sure must have a tongue!' He was worth every cent that cheque was made out for. He thought, 'If I told this guy Russ Farran was sitting next to him, I'll bet he'd insist on buying me a drink.' But he didn't risk it. He was safer unrecognised.

He asked, 'Who was that guy? The guy that spoke up for Farran?'

'His uncle — El Farran.'

Farran whistled soundlessly, watching Farranville grow around them. For until now he'd been thinking that it was his uncle El who was back of all his troubles.

8

He dropped off downtown, where most of his employees lived, and phoned from a bar a good two miles from Lacey's. That put one over the cops — they couldn't be listening in on that wire.

He asked for Miss Alyss Farran, but Darling McMee came to the phone. She sounded breathless, as if she had run all the way up some stairs.

'Alyss told me to come — she's outside making sure no one gets to hear what I'm saying. She said you'd probably prefer to speak to me, anyway.'

He did. His heart gave a quick leap when her voice came over the wire, and it kept on beating fast when he realised the girl didn't seem to be suspicious of him any more.

'You don't think I used that gun on Joe, do you, Darling?' he said quickly.

'No.'

'I could tell that by your voice. Thank God.'

'Alyss and I have been talking. And that showdown at the factory today proved you were right in saying somebody is out to smear your name.' He heard her laugh, but there was a little catch in it. 'Alyss was at the meeting. She's a shareholder, of course. She said he was wonderful, that big tramp you sent up. He just shouted everyone down and made them listen to him. He could talk and seemed to enjoy talking, Alyss said.'

Farran said, fervently, 'His name's Death, but he's put life into me, that fellow.'

'And Alyss says your uncle talked strongly for you, too. She says she had never expected it of him, but he really talked in your favour. Alyss thinks a lot of people who speak up for you, Russ.'

He said, 'I wanted to ask her about the meeting, but I guess that'll do. I've something to tell you, Darling.'

'Well?' Her voice was a little breathless still, but perhaps now it was because she knew he was going to tell her something very important.

'There are some of the old Detroit

Chopper organization mixed up in this strike. I can't figure out how yet, but they're hanging around.' She didn't say anything. 'Can't you see what that means, Darling?' he asked sharply.

And when she said, 'No,' he told her — 'Joe was the bloodhound that went trailing the Choppers, wasn't he? Suppose these Choppers here tumbled to it that he'd just come to L.A.? They might figure he was trailing them, yeah? All right, being Choppers they thought they knew a way of quieting him — a brutal way.'

'You think the Choppers shot him?'

'I think they're more likely to have done it than I. Joe sure was unlucky to open up office during the period of Farrans' labour troubles.'

'Poor Joe.' He heard her voice break, and he wished he'd kept Joe's name out of it. She'd thought a lot about her husband, he thought, and he found himself wishing there was someone in his life like that.

And that brought him round to Lydia — Lydia van Heuson. He didn't want to talk about her, especially for some reason didn't wish to explain to Darling McMee. But he thought he'd better; it had to come some time, anyway.

'About those photostats of letters found in my room — '

'That's all right, I've seen them.'

He was surprised; he hadn't thought of that happening so quickly. And he wasn't pleased because she had seen them. Lydia could be very, very amorous when she was trailing for another husband.

'Yes, Alyss and I went into L.A. early this morning to see the police on several matters. I convinced them the writing wasn't mine.'

'No.' He tried to think of some way around the subject, failed and so bluntly came out with the truth. 'They came from a girl I know; she collects husbands. I was down for about Number Four until I wised up to things. She wrote me a few times, making appointments, but she was cute enough to keep her name off the letters. Lydia knows all the answers I reckon.'

'Lydia?'

'You don't need to know who she is. All

I say is, if she hadn't come out of Macartney's when she did, I'd never have dropped into your office that day.'

He heard her voice softly over the wire, 'Then perhaps I should be very grateful to Lydia.'

He didn't say anything to that, so she went on. 'They showed me another letter down at police headquarters. It seemed to be intended for you but was never finished and never mailed.'

'Oh? Who wrote it?'

'Joe. It was on hotel paper where he stayed in Washington. We think he started to write it, then came home quickly and perhaps forgot it was in his wallet.'

'What was in the letter?'

'Nothing much. It said that he wanted to see you because he thought there was something you ought to know.'

Farran stared blankly at the mouth-piece before him, but it gave no inspiration. 'He never contacted me — he didn't have time, I suppose. I wonder what he wanted to tell me?'

'We can't guess . . . Perhaps it had nothing to do with your present problems.'

'You want my hunch? It had. Your Joe was a smart man; he must have figured out all that I'm just beginning to understand right now.'

They both stopped speaking. Both wanted to keep the other talking, to protract this conversation endlessly, yet it somehow languished.

Darling whispered, 'I hate to think of you on the run like this, Russ. You've inherited all the troubles of the world, it seems.' As if she didn't have her own. 'Can you — get out of them, do you think?'

'You want me to try?'

'Why, of course.'

He came to a decision. He'd been working around the idea for some time, but it was risky. Now he decided to risk all on a chance to establish his innocence.

'I think I might do it — tonight,' he said. 'But I want to speak to Alyss now, please.'

She said, 'Goodbye, Russ. Look after yourself.' And he said, 'Goodbye, Darling,' then wondered if he'd meant the word to start with a capital.

When Alyss came he told her something he didn't want Darling to know. 'If I can get into the factory tonight I know I can put the blame where it should be. I'm going in, Alyss.'

When she heard what he intended to do she was panicky. 'You'll get hurt. They'll catch you. The police are everywhere. Oh, Russ, look after yourself, dear. People are suddenly coming round to saying nice things about you!'

'So I've noticed,' Farran admitted 'So long as you think well of me, honey, that's enough.'

She interrupted, 'And Darling, also. She's a lovely person, Darling. You know, she's the kind of girl you ought to have met — not like Lydia and the others.' So she knew about those indiscretions, he thought humorously. 'Maybe in six months or a year — '

He stopped her. He didn't want her to express what he'd been finding himself thinking. 'You're too young for match-making,' he said quickly, and then rang off.

He found it easy to thumb a ride out to

the Farran works; there were a lot of strikers riding out.

'Looks like we'll be back soon,' his driver told him. 'They've called a big meeting for tonight. Don't know much about it myself, but they say there's industrial sabotage at the bottom of these strikes we've been having. It isn't that fellow Farran at all.'

Farran kept thinking of Alyss's words — 'People are suddenly coming round to saying nice things about you.' It was overwhelming — but he could take a lot more of it.

On the parking lot there was pandemonium. Half a dozen meetings were on at once, gigantic meetings, attended by thousands of sullen, angry workers. But the biggest meeting was one up by where the strike leader's caravan was parked, only he wasn't addressing it.

Over the sea of heads Farran saw the shambling bulk of Jim Death on top. He was in his element — he had an audience of three or four thousand people to listen to him, and he was making the best of it.

One word kept floating across to him

— 'suckers.' It came time after time, and each time he used it a low, angry growl went up from the throats of that big audience. Farran realised that the big hobo was deliberately working for an emotional reaction among his audience — and was getting it.

No man likes to be told that he has been led for a sucker for months on end, but that was what the tramp was telling them now.

'Lewen an' his pals have been spreading whispers agen the boss for months. They got you so you would believe anything against him, so you wouldn't trust him at all. They got you to stop work and strike time after time, and you suckers went and did it just as they wanted. Suckers!' Explosive contempt. 'You gave up your pay packets, but they went on getting theirs — only bigger ones.'

That thought got the men hopping mad.

'If you've any doubts,' shouted the yawp, 'see what the police report is on that letter Lewen stuck on the notice board last week.' He waved a paper in his hand, then read from it.

'"The signature attached to the letter submitted is undoubtedly a clever forgery".'

He bent and handed the police report to be passed from hand to hand among the crowd. There was no doubt from the reception that what he had read out was genuine.

A yell went up from the crowd, 'Where's Lewen?'

'Lewen?' Death made a derisive gesture. 'As soon as they heard what I had to say inside there, they skedaddled! There's none of 'em here, Lewen or his pals. But the police are after 'em for it, just like they're watching me now!'

Farran got it. The yawp was telling him he was a marked man and it was too dangerous for Farran to try to speak to him. He looked round. Back of the crowd were some uniformed cops, but he guessed that in addition there'd be detectives inconspicuously mingling with the men.

Then he heard the big yawp shout

something that made his heart jump.

'Yeah, the cops'll get Lewen, an' when they do it won't be nice for him. For why? Because the D.A.'s anxious to get him to say who's been putting out all this money to make labour trouble. And he'll talk! What they did to me this afternoon ain't nothing to what Lewen will get from a police grilling!'

So they'd put the yawp through it after the meeting, Farran thought. The cops would. He was lucky to be out right now . . .

He felt someone take his arms from behind. He went rigid.

A voice said softly, 'Come out of the crowd; don't make any fuss, see?'

Farran got his head round. There was a fellow right back of him, wearing just jeans and shirt like himself. He was big and there was curling hair on his chest.

Farran said, just as softly, 'What for? What do you want?'

The fellow looked significant. 'I've got something to say to you. Come on out.'

Farran started to follow, even then not suspecting the truth. He was saying to himself, 'Who can this fellow be?' while at the same time for some reason he connected him with the big yawp, Jim Death, up there bawling his unshaven face off atop the caravan.

Then he got it.

He looked at the hand that gripped him. It was big — big and strong. It looked the kind of hand that could do a lot of things and had done a lot. But not work. Not holding spanners or portable tools alongside a metal hull or anything like that. The skin was too soft and free from dirt for the hand to belong to a man who lived by his manual earnings.

Yet he was dressed for the part.

Farran smiled and said, 'You're a cop?'

The fellow smiled and said, 'Come outside an' I'll tell you.'

And at that he knew he was a cop.

Fury rose again inside Farran — a fury that was product of frustration. For it seemed that he had kept his freedom long enough to understand and to be able to plan so that other people might understand — and now he was to be put away where he couldn't go through with his plans. And if he couldn't do it, if it weren't entered upon without delay, then the opportunity would be lost . . . lost forever.

Farran ripped up his arms as well as the press of the crowd would let him, and the cop lost his grip. But Farran couldn't just turn and run at that; there were several thousand very solid men all around him.

The cop came back with a cruel hold on his wrist and forearm.

Around, men were stirring, growling protests, turning to watch the fight. Farran went berserk, thrashing with his left, using his body as a lever against the pain that held his right arm, and all the time they fought against a wall of barely-yielding, solid humanity that began to shout against the discomfort of their position.

The cop was shouting, too. Farran didn't know what he said, but it must have been a call for help, for suddenly there was another big, grinning bub shoving through and laying hands on him. And at that, even before a third came up, Farran knew they had him.

That didn't stop him from struggling. He wasn't the kind to give in while there was fight left in his body, and he gave those three big detectives a run for their money.

It stopped the speaker up there on the caravan. No speaker has ever yet been able to compete with a good brawl, and when he saw the attention of his audience diverted, the big, saggy yawp up top shut up his mouth and stood and watched.

And then a word came up to him, came rippling from mouth to mouth like a wisp of flame through dry September grass.

'It's Farran! The cops have got him!'

One of the cops had put the word out, knowing that a crowd won't stand by and see one man roughly handled by three. As soon as they started to get threatening the cop said, 'It's Farran. Make a way for us — we're police.'

He did it confidently, though he wasn't always confident about proclaiming his identity before a crowd of workpeople; because the things he had heard the men say against Russ Farran suggested they would be allies and not enemies.

They began to open up, to let the struggling quartet through. They were nearly out of the crowd, nearly out where a ton of beef in blue uniforms stood waiting to sling him into a police truck, when the voice of the yawp came bellowing over the din — 'They're not cops! It's another frame up!'

It was a dangerous thing to say, with all those police witnesses around but the yawp came out with it all the same. And his last words produced their effect, as he had guessed they would.

There'd been so many frame ups in which they had appeared as suckers that they just weren't going to stand for another one!

They didn't question how they stood with the captive, didn't ask if it was Farran, the man they had hated so much until the last hour or so. All they knew was they weren't going to find they'd been made suckers again.

The crowd surged, pressed forward and engulfed the protesting detectives. One moment they had a firm grip on their prisoner, the next he was torn from them like a drowning man is torn away by an angry sea. It was irresistible.

Farran found himself being borne forward in the struggling mass, separated from his captors. It was like an eddy in a whirlpool, the way he was taken round and round in an ever-widening circle within that huge crowd. And somehow he got lost in it.

At first the people around had known him for Farran, but then the movement carried him away even from them and suddenly he realised he was back where he started — an unknown in the midst of his workpeople.

He found the eddying movement dying down until finally the crowd was still again, still but murmuring . . . asking questions. And the principal question was — 'Where's Farran? What happened to him?'

Farran began to ask the question, too. He thought if he did people wouldn't take any notice of him, and it seemed to succeed. And the light wasn't as good as it had been.

The yawp started speaking again. He was telling them they ought to go back the next day and start negotiations afresh with the management. A loud roar of approval went up from the fed-up men, and at that Farran knew that the strike was broken. It seemed they were solidly behind their new labour leader, Jim Death.

And then another voice intervened, to drown even that yawping voice up on the caravan. It came from those big speakers over the gate.

'This is the police. There is a man in that crowd who is wanted on a charge of murder. His name is Russell Farran, and he owns this factory.'

The crowd went still and quiet, listening. Farran felt ice trickles run down his back.

'The meeting is entirely surrounded,' that deep, bellowing voice thundered out to them. 'Farran cannot escape through my cordon of men.'

Farran craned to see over the heads of the crowd. A blinding light fell on his face. It wasn't dark yet, but it was coming dusk and the police had fixed searchlights on top of their cars and were training them on the meeting. If he'd had any thought of escaping under cover of darkness, this seemed to sabotage things.

Then the appeal switched to him. 'Farran, come and give yourself up quietly. You can't get away — we won't let you!'

No, they'd do their damnedest to catch him. The police will go through hell to get the killer of one of their men.

But Farran didn't move. Instead he was looking at that big yawp, stuck up against the darkening sky. And the yawp didn't seem to know what to do, either.

He just stood and waited, and the minutes passed. Minutes of silence uncanny with so many men standing there, brilliantly illuminated in the white glare of searchlights.

Then he seemed to get fed up. He started to climb down. And at once a murmur went through the crowd. 'The meeting's over. Back to work tomorrow.'

Now, the police can watch for one man to break away from a crowd, like a rabbit that bolts from the last standing strip of corn before the reaper gets to it. But it can't do much when a crowd suddenly disintegrates — suddenly erupts and spreads out in every direction at once.

As it did now.

As soon as the word got round, that crowd suddenly remembered a hundred important things it had forgotten, like having a meal or having a drink or even just going home and getting their aching feet up.

They went in a rush for their cars so as to be first out, while others piled down to the road in order to thumb a lift. Farran went with the latter. As he shoved his way along with the suddenly vociferous crowd he wondered if the yawp had anticipated this, had deliberately engineered the whole thing. Could be — he was a very wide-awake man . . . too wide-awake to bother about work when there were more exciting things to do.

He went with the crowd, pushing round against it so that he came up alongside that long, high, wire-mesh fence that circled the huge works. When the fence left the road he dodged down a path alongside it until he came to a small gate that was always locked but which had once been a private entrance for the Farran family when the first office block stood this side of the works. He still had a key to it.

There was no one following up that little-used pathway. He heard the roar of accelerating cars, the hubbub of talking, shouting men. Saw shafts of light streak across the nearly dark sky as the searchlights moved into new positions of vantage. But no one seemed to be watching him.

He went quickly through the gate, and then hid behind a battery of cooling pipes until he was sure he hadn't been followed. When he was certain he went into the biggest of the Service Blocks, the nerve centre of the entire works. He had to break a window to get in — but he got in.

Once inside he worked quickly, using his pocketknife as a screwdriver. He spent most of his time tracing cables, but once traced it didn't take long for him to change the connections . . .

When that was done be went outside into the long deserted avenues. There would be watchmen about the works, he knew, but he also knew that if he went carefully he didn't stand much chance of being seen.

He went clambering among the shunting tracks, dodging between the long, silent rows of stationary rail cars. A moon was lifting back over the Mojave Desert, not a big one but it gave sufficient light.

It was a long way round, through the yards, but for some reason he felt he had plenty of time. He had expected that electrical work to take longer, but it had gone nicely . . .

He was still a long way from the Administration Block when he heard cars approaching — several cars; saw their headlights rise and dip as they came over the hill just within the gates.

He froze. Now he realised how uncertain his plans had been. Vaguely he had expected a result, but he hadn't thought in detail how that result would manifest itself. For instance, for some reason he had expected only one car to come through those gates, not several. Afterwards he couldn't understand why he'd thought like that; logically it could have been expected.

He stood, stiff as an obsolete aircraft propeller, in the shadow of a tall freight car, his eyes probing, his ears listening.

He heard the engines die and from the sound they were outside the Administration Block. The headlights, reflecting from a distant high concrete wall, snapped out. Then there was silence again.

Farran didn't move for minutes after that, debating what to do. Several cars meant many people, and many people was something he hadn't reckoned on. Especially if they were police.

The thought jolted him. If they were police then his suspicions were unfounded. That meant he was still as far as ever from clearing himself . . . it meant that he had made a trap for himself.

Yet in time he came round to the idea of going forward, just as he had planned it originally. Perhaps it was recklessness that prompted the decision — perhaps despair.

He came out from the shelter of the shadowy trucks and ran quickly across a patch of moonlight towards the nearest of the big office buildings.

As he ran into the gloom he realised they had been waiting for him.

9

Perhaps they hadn't actually been expecting him, perhaps they just happened to be there — just a little more of the jinx that had dogged Farran these last days.

He saw them as shadows, heard a gasp of surprise.

There were two of them; two men just coming round the corner. When they saw him, both came jumping forward, both pulling things out of their pockets.

Farran was running when he saw them and it gave him an advantage. He was moving too quickly for them, moving faster than they could get their hands up. He jumped, and there was fury and desperation behind the leap. His plan seemed to be going all to hell right from the start, didn't seem as if it would work out at all.

So he went for those crouching men — and Farran had been a big, tough quarterback in his college days and knew all about charging a man.

They went down before his weight, and he heard something metallic hit the concrete apron round the office base. He hoped it was a gun come adrift. A knee came up into his stomach, a hand shoved into his face and kept stabbing with the hard heel of it into his nose, hurting and bringing the smell of blood to him. And someone was grappling, trying to throw him over on to his back.

He used his left in a series of short jabs to a body that grunted and yielded and went back quickly as though it hurt; his feet came round and started to hack at feet that were kicking out at him.

It was a dogfight, a bitchy, snarling, ferocious affair of half a minute.

And even in the midst of it, Farran had a feeling — these weren't cops — one of the guys was too small for that. It brought exhilaration to him; perhaps he could bring off his plan, after all!

A gun waved towards his skull, striking out at him. He took only half the blow, pulling his head back quickly. Savagely he tore at the gun hand, trying to wrest it from that clinging hand. Deliberately, because both hands were occupied with that gun, be threw himself into a roll and that detached the second fellow from his back.

They were panting, breath coming in gasps, because brawling like that is a quickly-tiring affair. Then the gun came away in his grip . . . and he dropped it.

He rolled on to his knees, struggling against those clinging arms that strove to hold him on the ground. That fellow was riding his back again, was trying to find his eyes with hooked fingertips. Farran had the other man before him, had him by the throat with his left hand. For the second the unknown was at his mercy and he wanted to take fullest advantage of it. He kept thumping with his right fist, smashing it into that face.

He heard gasps, felt warm blood on his hand, then quick groans as his swift-flailing fist cut open that helpless face.

And then he couldn't stand the gouging any more and he stooped and shot the rider from his back, and as the man came over he rolled with him, getting his weight on top of him. It meant letting go of the other fellow, but there was nothing else for it.

Somehow they all staggered clear of each other after that. Farran, coming immediately up from his knees, saw the one whose face had been pounded. He was reeling towards something bright that lay on the concrete just beyond the black line of shadow.

Farran thought, 'He's not feeling good, that rube,' and concentrated on him.

The second man was in at him again, flailing with fists that hurt every time they landed — he was snarling. But Farran ignored him, ignored him as much as you can ignore a man who is hurting you badly. He drove into the reeling opponent, hitting him savagely, knocking him round and hitting him again. He heard those moans rise again and knew he had hurt the man badly, and it filled him with ferocious triumph and he laced into his opponent and battered him until he folded up hard against the concrete apron. He stopped moaning then.

Farran went staggering forward from

the force of his attack, came sliding on to his knees again. Then he found that his hand was within inches of a gun butt, and he reached out and grabbed it.

He rolled on to his side, so that he could cover the other opponent, and his gun came up. He was lying out in the moonlight now, and the fellow would see that gun clearly.

He did. It stopped the rush that was coming. He stopped just where he was, just how he was, one foot poised ready for a brutal kick.

Farran panted from the ground, 'That's it, stop like that.' He hadn't strength for a second to lift himself from the ground.

Then he saw the shadowy figure step a pace backwards into the darker shadows. He snarled, 'Keep still or I'll drill you.' But he was bluffing, he daren't use that gun and maybe the other fellow knew it.

He went on going backwards, step after step, and Farran came swaying to his feet after him. The unknown got to the corner, turned it and disappeared. When Farran came up he was in time to see the rube go clattering hell for leather across more rail tracks towards the maintenance Block. He let him go. He stood there, considering what to do.

Then something occurred to him. That fellow had run away without shouting for help, as you'd expect a man to do if he was within the works on lawful business. Farran cast his mind back to that struggle in the shadows — it had been a comparatively noiseless affair, too. He thought, 'Those fellows don't want people to know they're around.' But he couldn't think why.

He leaned against the wall and rubbed his aching eyes. He wouldn't need to rub tobacco in them now, he thought ironically; they'd be nice and bloodshot tomorrow without that . . .

A sound from behind brought him wheeling. That other opponent must have been plenty tough, for he had got up, sneaked over and found the second gun and was coming up behind Farran with murder on his bruised and bleeding face.

He wasn't considering the consequences of noise, that hombre. He had a gun; he was hurt and he intended to use that gun on the fellow who had hurt him. Farran.

Farran ran for it, because though he had a gun himself he couldn't use it. He of all people had to keep quiet that night.

He must have hurt that gunman badly, for when he led him across more tracks the fellow seemed not to see them and he stumbled and went down very hard, and after that only managed to crawl a yard or two before collapsing completely.

Farran saw it from the back of the Administrative Block, but he didn't go back to the fellow. Instead he used his key and passed inside the huge, silent building.

Silent — but he knew someone was there. He walked warily but openly down a moonlit corridor, climbed some stairs in preference to making a noise with the elevator, and came out on the senior executives' floor. There was a light under one of the doors. He didn't need to ask whose.

He went, gun in hand, opened the door and let it swing wide.

Uncle El was sitting behind his massive

desk. Only his desk light was on, so that he sat, a great, bulking form, in a pool of yellow light in that otherwise big, dark room.

Farran went in, saw the room was empty apart from Uncle El, and shut and locked the door behind him. He didn't want interruptions.

Then he came slowly across towards the desk. The gun was dangling from his hand. He wondered if his uncle could recognise him. He hadn't shaved for nearly two days now, and there was blood all over his face. His cropped hair, torn shirt and soiled jeans, wouldn't be any aids to identity, either.

But he knew Uncle El had recognised him as soon as the thought came into his mind. Uncle El wouldn't have sat silent if a hobo had burst into the room.

Farran said, ' 'Lo, Uncle El.' Always he called him that, and many of the workpeople had got it from him now. He thought sometimes El didn't like it; big tycoons these days preferred the fashion of initials, and probably, secretly, he'd have liked to hear people calling, 'Oh,

E.J . . . ' Elmer J. Farran certainly fancied himself as a man of commercial and industrial might.

Uncle El just sat and said nothing. The light glistened from a yellow skin that seemed greasy, reflecting pronounced highlights; and it came back from those thick-lensed, rimless big-businessman's glasses so that to Farran he seemed to have two blank white eyes. Farran looked at the thick, bloodless lips in that heavy-jowled face and waited for them to speak. When it was obvious that Uncle El didn't intend to speak, Farran spoke again.

'Alyss told you I wanted to see you?' It could be that that big head nodded slightly. Nodded, didn't speak. And it was vital that he should be made to speak. He'd got to make him speak . . .

And then, right when he was feeling that he was near to triumph, he remembered something. Remembered something he should have thought of before but hadn't. After all this, his scheme was a flop, a waste of time!

Because he realised that Jim Death had

spoilt everything, had sabotaged his plans for him.

It was funny. Right when he realised that it didn't matter what Uncle El said now, Uncle El up and spoke and said everything just as he'd hoped he'd say it. That was just like life, full of ironies, he thought.

'What do you want with me? Why did you ask me to meet you here?'

In bitterness Farran nearly walked out on him then, nearly passed up the whole abortive plan. Because he answered the questions was only because he couldn't think where else to go and what else to do.

He said, 'I wanted to know why you were making so much trouble for me?'

Uncle El told him, his voice level and monotonous and as full of music as a stone-cruncher. 'Because I'm more fit to be head of Farrans than anybody. And you're not. You got to the top not by ability but because your father left you the works. But I helped your father rise from obscurity to become one of the giants of American industry. I . . . made him what he was.'

'You made him?' Farran laughed grimly. No one had made the old man except his own, brilliant self.

'Yeah, I made him.' Uncle El sat like a fat, unemotional yellow idol, absolutely sure in what he was saying, flatly certain that what he said was the divine truth. And Farran watched him curiously, because in these last days he had begun to understand Uncle El.

'Good relations with labour is the key to success today. I always handled that side for your father, and I was acknowledged the best labour relations officer in the country.'

'Until,' reminded Farran, 'about a year ago. Since when your record stinks.' He wished they had witnesses to this conversation.

Uncle El ignored the crack. 'I made Farrans because I kept peace within the firm. I could have gone on keeping peace with labour, but when your father died and you stepped into his place — ' He paused.

'You quit,' said Farran. 'Didn't you?

You've always wanted to be top dog, always thought you were smart enough to be boss of the outfit. You knew you couldn't put anything over the old man while he was alive and you probably never even tried it. But you thought differently about me, didn't you? You had a contempt for me — you have a contempt for most people, haven't you, Uncle El? You think you're smart enough to lick any human being, don't you?'

'I've spent my life meeting men and beating 'em. What I don't know about men isn't worth knowing.' He said it so tonelessly that even Farran didn't realise the enormity of that brag. If he had he would have realised how near to being a monomaniac his self-centred, highly-opinionated relative was.

'So about a year ago you decided to put men against men, intending to come out on top and be king of Farrans, huh?'

And then Farran stopped, because he thought he had heard a rustling noise. He looked again quickly round the big office, but it was empty. Just the usual office furniture. Windows, but they were closed against the night. And only one door and that was locked and the key was in the lock so that nobody else could open it from outside.

Uncle El droned on, 'Sure I did. And I'm glad you arranged this meeting, Russ. I've always wanted you to know what I've been doing to you, how I've outsmarted you.'

'You've hated me because I was over you, haven't you?'

Uncle El lifted a fat, heavy hand as if to rub out the words. 'Hate? Bah, how can you hate something you despise?'

'All right, you despised me. You set about getting me in jake with one lot of people or another. And you did it cleverly.'

'I do everything cleverly,' those fat lips told him humourlessly. 'I got us into the power of the bank by approving of schemes which required us to borrow money. And then I made the bank uneasy about their money, let them think it wasn't a good investment while you were running the show.'

'Yeah, I've guessed most of that now,'

said Farran. In fact he knew it all, pretty nearly all, anyway, and wasn't even bothered to hear Uncle El corroborate it.

'You got labour distrustful of me. It was easy — you were labour relations officer and you were able to get your stooges like Lewen to shout every time they heard the boss's name mentioned. I always thought those strikes didn't add up, somehow.'

There was only one thing really puzzled him. Where did the Chopper Boys fit into the picture? So he came out with the question.

Big, fat Uncle El brooded for a time, as if trying to recall a difficult circumstance of events. 'I was going to use them to make the biggest, ugliest strike we'd had. I was going to introduce them into the works as scab labour — '

'I get it. Making out I'd put 'em there, huh?'

Uncle El nodded. 'I knew the men wouldn't stand for it; they'd come piling in and there'd be fighting. The Choppers were instructed not to pull punches — I wanted men hurt, maybe men killed.'

'Meaning me to stand the bill?'

Farran's face was grim. It was a cunning plot and it had nearly succeeded. So Alyss had been right in what she had told him that day when he'd come home with Darling. He couldn't think how she'd known, but had wished he'd bothered to question her further. Probably she'd overheard some conversation with one of the Choppers — or maybe a telephone call.

'You're pretty sure of yourself, talking openly about getting men killed?' Farran's hand tightened on his gun. He didn't trust this fat man; suddenly he was uneasy, because it was all too simple, getting a confession like this from him. It would have been fine, just as he had planned it, but for the yawp ending the strike and sending everyone home. *He'd forgotten that.*

Uncle El's flat, monotonous voice said, 'Getting men killed doesn't mean a thing to me. Men are fools, anyway. A clever man just uses men. A really clever man knows when not to use them.'

Farran heard that rustling sound again; this time he was certain. And yet he was baffled because apart from Uncle El and himself that room seemed empty. He listened tensely, ready to act.

And nothing happened.

Uncle El's voice just droned on: 'Like the Choppers. I pulled 'em out just when I'd planned to use 'em. And why? Because I saw I could get rid of you without clumsy labour brawls. You gave me a great break, Russ, that day when you walked on to McMee's corpse and pulled suspicion on to yourself. I figured from that moment you could change the boss's chair for an electric one.'

'You're a fine uncle for a man to have!'

'I don't go for silly sentiment.' Those blank, codfish eye-glasses moved and the light stopped reflecting for an instant and he saw pale grey eyes behind them. And in those eyes, as sure as anything, there was the light of mania. His uncle was a crackpot, obsessed with the desire for power and determined at all costs to get it.

'When I want a thing I go for it. I wanted your job, and I'm going to get it, Russ. I shan't have any regrets, either, the way you go out.'

'So I'm due to go out?'

'Sure.' That big head nodded, and Farran saw the folds of flesh ride up and down the tight collar. 'You don't think I can let you live, do you? I've found a job for the Choppers tonight.'

Farran understood. 'You came in with them? They're all over the works. What's it this time for them — sabotage in addition to playing executioner to me?' He wished he could spot where that rustling came from.

'No sabotage.' The heavy head nodded emphatically. 'I want an efficient works when I take over. Just you. They've been told not to let you get out of this place alive, Russ. You'll simply disappear — your body will never be found — and with a nice show of reluctance I'll allow myself to be elected into your position.'

'And when they catch up with Lewen and make him talk?'

'I've got so much on Lewen he daren't talk,' said Uncle El simply, and Farran knew he wasn't exaggerating there.

He thought he'd localised that rustling

sound. It seemed to come from a big steel cupboard along one side of the room. It didn't look deep enough to be able to contain a man, but all the same Farran began to think it might. He watched it out of the corners of his eyes, waited for the next rustling sound.

'You didn't know Joe McMee was an ex-F.B.I. man?' Darling had told him that. Joe wouldn't use his past record to help him with his enquiry agency. He was a modest man, but probably that piece of modesty had caused his brains to be blown out.

Uncle El sighed. His hand was reaching out for a switch on his intercom system. Farran thought, 'He's going to call in the Choppers. Doesn't he know I've got a gun — and mean to use it?'

That flat, gravelly voice: 'I didn't know. You should have told me.' His voice sounded hurt in a curious child-like way. 'I'd heard of the man behind the Choppers; I'd got a clue that he'd been seen in a place in Washington. Your college friend traced him for me.'

Then, thought Farran, Joe must have

tumbled to it who the fellow was. He'd started to write to him to give him the tip, then he'd come back in a hurry, but before he could communicate with Farran a Chopper had come along and ended his life.

'A Chopper killed Joe?' Even if the world outside wasn't getting this broadcast, he wanted to know for his own satisfaction.

'Sure, it was a Chopper. Joe McMee was recognised in Washington. The Chopper chief thought he was tailing them still and he had McMee followed and put out.'

'And from then on you worked to put the blame on me?'

It was all too easy, too obvious.

'You put that gun into my room?'

'Sure.' Uncle El was twiddling with the intercom switch. Farran watched with brooding satisfaction.

'And the ape?' He wanted to know everything while he was at it. 'That detective called Mulhoney?'

Uncle El twiddled again. 'The one who got burned up?' Farran nodded. 'He recognised one of the Choppers. It was a fool who was hanging around to see what was happening at the McMee office. Me, I wouldn't have done such a damn' fool thing, but these Choppers don't run much to brain.'

'He decided to give us a rest and see what the Chopper was up to — the ape, I mean?'

'Sure.' Uncle El pounded the top of the intercom experimentally but didn't get any answer. And yet he seemed only very mildly bothered by it. 'But the Chopper saw he was being tailed and he ran the cop into the arms of some of his friends. They handled him badly back off the road before he'd stop fighting and let himself be burned up. They didn't think at the time that crime would be laid to your account as well, Russ.' He almost chuckled. Everything had suited him. Everything. Even Russ Farran sending word through he wanted to meet him after dark inside the lonely factory.

Farran watched that twiddling fat forefinger and finally said, 'It won't work, Uncle El.'

His uncle withdrew his finger and swivelled that big head round on his thick neck. His glasses reflected a sightless stare.

Farran said gently, 'You can't call in your Choppers, Uncle El, because I did things to your intercom about half an hour ago.'

Uncle El sat slowly back in his chair. But it still didn't make sense to Farran. Uncle El was no fool and he could surely see that that gun would get him before he could bring help in through that locked door. Maybe, he thought, in planning all this he hadn't expected Farran to be armed. That could be upsetting the whole trap . . .

Uncle El said, 'What have you done to the wiring?'

'I connected it right through to the public address system outside the gates. The one you had fixed up so as to be able to put across the firm's point of view, as you used to call it.'

Uncle El was as still as any man ever could be short of being a corpse. Then he put his finger on the weakness of the plot, and Farran knew that his bluff hadn't fooled his uncle.

'You wanted me to broadcast a public confession, only you picked the wrong day for it. Yesterday, the day before, and a lot of days before that — yes. But not tonight. Why? Because the car park's empty. All the strikers are at home or in movies or bars. The P.A. System's been talking to thin air — if it has been talking at all,' he ended significantly.

Farran tried one last bluff. 'It has been talking — or I'm no electrician. And you've forgotten one thing — the gate police.'

Uncle El began to rise out of his chair.

'The gate police are a hundred yards back of the speakers. They'll hear a noise, but not a word of what's being said. They're inside the fence and they won't go out because it's not their duty to go out. Anyway, they're used to hearing it and will only think it's being tested.'

Farran said, sincerely, 'You're as smart a man as any I've ever met, Uncle El.'

'Smarter,' said his uncle. 'I wasn't going to call anyone on that intercom system. I just wanted to keep your eyes this way. I hate to see men carrying guns like you're doing.'

And when Farran turned he saw a Chopper standing inside that big steel cupboard. The oiled door hinges were opening silently. The Chopper had a sub-automatic in his bands.

And Farran remembered that in the argot of the underworld another name for a machine gun was — a chopper.

10

Aloud he said, 'I'm a sucker.' The chopper menaced and he let his automatic slip to the floor. This time he didn't need to be told what to do and his hands climbed above his head.

Uncle El stubbed a desk button. His voice was as flat as ever, though he had triumphed after all. 'To be really smart Russ, you've got to think well ahead of your fellow men. I just happen to be born smart. Now go to the door, unfasten it and see what we have outside for you.'

Farran went slowly across to the door. He was thinking, 'This is it. There'll be a corridor full of Choppers. It'll be the beginning of a long walk for me.'

So he didn't hurry. He let his hands come down very slowly at the door, let his fingers turn the key as if there was a prize for slow-motion work. But however long he took in the end it was done, and then he had to turn the door handle and let it swing open.

Framed in the doorway was a man.

A big man.

A man with a blue scrub chin and rough red face.

A man whose stomach sagged over his belted pants, whose clothes looked weary, as if they'd been slept in — often.

The yawp. *Jim Death himself!*

'The bearer's name is — ' he heard himself shouting. He was bewildered, this was past comprehension. What was the yawp doing here? Was the yawp a Chopper himself . . . the Chief Chopper? A thousand wild, chaotic thoughts flooded into his brain, a tangled, knotted skein that wouldn't unravel in a matter of seconds.

And he wasn't even given that length of time. Maybe be had only half a second at that.

For a familiar voice was yawping — 'Run, bub! Run!'

A big hand was reaching and grabbing and tossing him out into the passage.

Then hell burst its banks. The chopper

stuttered into a sharp murderous burst of life — lead screamed and flattened into the corridor woodwork, gouging out long thick splinters, ripping holes in the polished panelling.

Farran fell along towards the stairs, but in stumbling he brought his head round. Back along the corridor, just outside Uncle El's secretary's room, two hoods stood with hands lifted above lowering, savage faces. The yawp was covering them with a stubby automatic. It made Farran wonder, even at the time. How come a yawp to have an automatic just when it was needed? But he was glad of it.

The yawp was running backwards after him, covering the two men. They'd be Choppers — two more of the gang, Farran knew.

He turned at the head of the stairs. The man with the chopper came out of Uncle El's room at that moment and started up with his gun. Farran saw his uncle close up behind the Chopper. Uncle El was carrying a revolver — maybe that revolver he'd dropped by the desk.

The yawp knocked him down the

stairs, trying to get off the landing before the sub started chattering. They rolled down the stairs together, and the roar of gunfire was deafening in their ears.

When they hit the bottom they started running. Farran realised that Death didn't know his way around, and he shouted, 'Follow me, blue beard!'

They went out. Back of them was silence now. Farran slowed. 'Watch out. Several car loads of Choppers came in. I guess they're all over the place searching for me.'

They lit out for the shunting yard, with its cover of freight cars. They were just running into them when every light in the place came up — the huge, ten thousand watt lamps that lit the yards and avenues as bright almost as day.

Uncle El didn't overlook anything. That light was just what the Choppers were needing.

Panting, they crawled under the rods and lay watching to see which way danger might come. Farran saw a form huddled among the tracks, and remembered that second Chopper he'd fought with who'd gone down heavily.

Jim Death alongside him got a chestful of breath and jerked, 'I got my gun from him. Comin' in.'

There was movement back along the Maintenance Block. Farran watched and whispered, 'When I saw you standing in the doorway I thought you were a Chopper. God, my heart stopped!'

The yawp was fumbling frantically inside his shirt. 'My heart stopped, too. I was listening outside that door when I heard a bell sound next office to it.' That would be Uncle El pressing that button. 'Next minute two boys come out — both Choppers.'

'But you had the drop on them?'

'You should have seen their faces.' The yawp was coming out with a familiar piece of paper. 'This is getting worth something, brother,' he yawped. 'How 'bout anteing up a bit more? Make it worth, say — fifty thousand?'

Farran reached for it. He wasn't going to argue. He wrote and initialled in the words 'Pay bearer fifty thousand dollars,' and didn't think any more about it.

Because the yawp had saved his life and that couldn't be measured in terms of dollars.

And anyway the cheque wasn't any use to him even so because if he wasn't killed right soon by the Choppers, in the end the police would get him and he knew he had nothing on Uncle El that would stand in court.

The shadows were moving, coming across now. Choppers. Five of them, crouching, guns in hand.

Farran thought, 'The gate police'll hear.'

Well, what would they hear? Guns going off in the works. And when they came round to it they'd find a corpse but no Choppers. The Choppers would disappear, but the corpse wouldn't because it couldn't.

And he would be the corpse.

'Yeah,' he started to say aloud, 'Uncle El wants me to be rubbed out.'

Then the yawp breathed, 'The hell, quit talkin' to yourself. Look, some more gunnies comin'!'

A couple had come round the corner

from the Admin Block. One looked to be carrying the chopper, but the other . . . Farran said, admiringly, 'Bless his guts, here's Uncle El. Kill him, you big yawp — kill him for me!'

The yawp blazed off — twice. Uncle El skipped quickly back around the corner. The yawp said regretfully, 'They don't jump like that if they're carryin' lead, I reckon.'

A bullet spattered on the steelwork above their heads, flattened and dropped between them. Farran touched it and found it too hot to hold. Then, as if with one mind, both rolled from under the freighter and belted hell for leather across to the loading bays.

When the chopper opened up, spraying that freighter, they weren't there — just.

The shadowy figures were coming across the track at a dozen different points now, flitting from truck to truck, and getting nearer. Farran realised there was no way round the loading building, and dashed for the wide steel doors.

He tried his keys in the lock of a small door inset into the bigger ones. None fitted by a mile. And there was no future in trying to pull a hole into those big doors, either.

The yawp busted a window and went through as the firing opened up again. Farran got hit in the calf, but it didn't stop him and must have been a mere snick. He fell in on top of the yawp.

It was still pretty light inside that quarter-mile-long building, with its row of loading bays where the trucks and rail cars came together. Farran saw several freight cars, just where they'd been left when the strike was called, and two or three powerful trucks, part loaded at the bays.

The yawp shouted, 'Where now?'

Farran wasn't sure but he kept on running. His idea was to cut through the adjacent filling station and somehow get out the back way. But when they came to where the long line of gasoline pumps stood with their up-looped guns and hoses, he saw men coming through another window alongside the filling station doors.

Farran went back quickly before he was seen. He stood back of a gas pump and hoped he wouldn't be spotted. The yawp got up behind the next one.

Farran said, 'Too bad you'll never cash that cheque.'

He heard a sigh. 'Too bad.' Then, wistfully, 'I've never believed it, anyway, fellar. You don't come by dollars so easy. There just had to be a snag.'

The Choppers were coming stealthily across behind them now, searching methodically through that long loading shed. They were so near they could see them, dodging almost soundlessly from cover to cover, yet always advancing.

And the hoods who had entered by the filling station door were coming round and across to join them.

Farran whispered, with grim humour, 'So what, fellar? It'd have been no use to you if we'd got out of this. The cops'd be waiting for me outside — '

Death exclaimed, 'The cops. Holy gee, I'd forgotten 'em!'

Farran got the excitement in his voice. 'The cops — ?'

'Sure, they should be here any minute now.'

'You sent for 'em?'

He saw that heavy, blue-chinned face break into a grin. 'Nope. Guess you sent for 'em, brother!'

So Farran said the obvious, 'You come again?'

Those silent figures were concentrating upon a pile of sacks right up where some building repairs were going on at the blank end of the station. It looked a more obvious place to hide than a line of gasoline pumps. Farran peeked round, about to make a dash for a window while their attention was distracted, then saw the sinister silhouette of the gunnie with the chopper up alongside those windows.

So he came back. He was wishing he had a gun like Jim Death's. It wasn't so bad, going out, if you could take someone with you.

Death was answering his question, gun aiming at a bulky figure standing back to watch the search against the blank wall.

'You get privileges when you become a labour leader — or you take 'em. Like that caravan. When I stepped into

Lewen's job I inherited his boudoir along with it.'

Farran's head began to come around, trying to work out the implications.

'You were out there when the public address system started to operate?'

'I was catchin' up on sleep.' The yawp was taking careful aim. 'I heard your uncle's voice so plain I never missed a syllable.'

'My God,' thought Farran. 'If only there'd been a few hundred strikers on tonight to witness it, too!' But there hadn't — only Jim Death, and his word wouldn't be any good because he was too closely identified with Farran. He groaned. So near — yet so very far away from clearing himself.

'You came in to help me out, then?' That was something he should always be grateful for.

'Yeah.' The bulky figure near the blank end of the shed stepped behind a concrete support. The yawp regretfully laid down his gun. 'But I did somep'n else first.'

'What?' It couldn't be important,

anyway, Farran thought. The search was ending back along that wall. Now the Choppers were coming back towards them. This was a job after their own hearts.

'I got through to the L.A. police H.Q. They'd fitted up that caravan with a phone so's Lewen didn't have to go home to talk to his wife. I said, 'Just get a load of this', and left the receiver on the doorstep.'

It was stunning, the thought that leapt into Farran's mind when he heard that.

'You don't mean — '

'I sure do. I'll bet they took down every word that was said, back in L.A. An' I'll bet they've a coupla hundred cops streaking up to Farrans right now.'

Farran took a deep breath. 'Then I'm not going under, Brother, I tell you I'm going to get out of here alive! They're not going to kill me, do you hear?'

The yawp said, 'All along I've never departed from that intention.' There were times when that yawp didn't talk a bit like a hobo.

Someone saw them, right at that

minute, and belted off a couple of rounds. They hurt the wall behind them a lot. The yawp saw a lot of figures running and pulled trigger. It stopped the advance, sent the mob back under cover by the sacks along the blank end wall. But the yawp suddenly turned and with tragic face said, 'This gun won't hurt anyone now. It's — empty!'

Far away — very far away — they heard the sound of a siren screaming. Too far away. When that mob heard the noise they'd come forward quickly to rub them out, and now they hadn't a gun to defend themselves with . . .

Hadn't they?

Farran suddenly had a gun. He jerked it up off the overhead clip, pressed the trigger and got the stink of raw gasoline in his nostrils. A stream of spirit shot out towards the advancing gunnies. It didn't hit them, but it was surprising how far that jet sprayed.

It stopped the Choppers. They'd never had that kind of gun turn on them before.

The yawp called, 'What'n hell?' Then Farran shouted to the mob, 'That's gasoline. You're all standing in it now, I reckon. The first man to fire a gun ignites the lot, I reckon.'

So no one fired. No one did anything except stand and look at that wetness that flooded all about them. No one could think what to do.

For Farran was pointing out, 'We're all trapped. We all go out together if this gas takes fire.' They were in the blank end of the building, right across from the doors and windows and the opening into the loading shed.

Outside the sirens were so loud now they all heard them. To make a noise like that they must have been inside the works. Farran thought, 'It'll make these monkeys do something quickly.'

But then he turned and saw the yawp was on the move away from him.

He was walking quite openly through the gasoline towards where a truck was standing, just where it had been left when the driver climbed out of the cab, to join the strike.

The yawp swung up. The Choppers came to life at that — or perhaps the police sirens woke them up. In a sudden surge they started to slop against the river of gasoline, coughing as the heavy fumes hit their throats.

Farran shouted desperately, 'Keep back,' and they hesitated, because they thought he might have the gun — and didn't know it was empty, anyway.

Then the truck thundered into life. The yawp took a chance on igniting the whole shed, and it came off. The truck came forward with a lurch.

So did the Choppers. They still didn't use their guns, however, still daren't. But they saw a way of catching their quarry, of settling things without danger to themselves.

Farran saw it just as the huge truck lurched alongside him. A fat, bulky figure was in the opening between the loading shed and the filling station. It was Uncle El and Uncle El was pointing a gun right at them. And Uncle El was a long way clear of the liquid gasoline.

It looked as though Uncle El suddenly had the whiphand, because if they tried to get out through that opening they just ran straight on to his gun.

But they did it, all the same, because the alternative was a mob of murderous Choppers.

Farran swung up and the truck went on without any slackening of speed. The Choppers skidded through the gasoline, trying to grab hold of the truck.

High up in the cabin, Farran and the yawp looked down to where the fat man stood. His hand was up, the gun pointing. They had a vision of a big-business tycoon, heavy of face and seemingly unemotional behind his glasses — unemotional, though he was — playing his last hand.

Then the yawp ducked down behind the wheel. Farran followed his example, and immediately the windscreen shattered and glass fell down on top of them.

There was no second shot.

A mighty roar came from behind them. Farran had heard the sound before — 'Whoosh!' A gasoline explosion. Something had ignited that gasoline-saturated atmosphere, either a backfire or that shot from Uncle El.

A column of flame was all around

them, there was an intense heat burning their hair and crisping the skin already, and a blast came circling round and knocked the breath out of their lungs. If they hadn't been in the shelter of that cab they could hardly have survived.

They jerked upright immediately. Farran had a glimpse of something just milling in front of the truck and then they went over an awkward bump. He wondered if Uncle El was alive when they hit him. If he had been, he couldn't be now. Not with that weight rolling across him.

Then they got snagged up in the tracks and ended against a truck.

The heat was intense, the flames licking after them like greedy, reaching hands. They didn't speak, just covered their faces and went tumbling out to the ground. Then they staggered through the loading bays until they came up against the big steel doors.

Their eyes were gumming up with the heat, their lips cracking. Above the roar of leaping flames Farran shouted, 'Any minute those pumps'll go up. Find a window!'

Then he plunged off along those

mighty doors. It seemed years before he came to a window, lurched against it with his shoulder and then pulled himself out.

On the ground, gulping great cool lungfuls of air, he turned his aching eyes out into the avenue. Cars were screaming up towards him, clearly illuminated in the big lights that Uncle El had switched on. Police cars. The next there'd be firemen . . . and ambulances.

He saw someone trying to struggle out of another window farther along, and though the heat was awful he went across to pull him out.

And it was a Chopper. Still alive. That was always the amazing thing about these big blazes — how men incredibly managed to survive in spite of everything.

But he was the only Chopper to get out of that place alive, and he wasn't much alive himself at that moment.

He got frantic then, trying to find the yawp. He was still staggering along from window to window when a couple of cops came racing across, hands shielding their faces from the heat, and dragged him away.

He was moaning, 'That hobo fellar. He's in there. Get him out. I want him to cash that cheque.'

But he was too far gone to resist and they pulled him away and carried him to a place of safety. A couple of minutes later, half the filling station blew up. It made a good funeral pyre for a lot of no-good hoodlums and also for a no-good power-mad man who had been Russ Farran's Uncle El.

They gave him water to drink, sitting him on a bench outside the Admin Block. And then Alyss was with him, and Darling McMee.

He gave a cracked grin. He knew he looked a hell of a mess, as much a hobo as old Jim Death, but he wasn't caring about appearances right then. He was alive. Even the absence of Death couldn't altogether dull the edge of the delight that that knowledge brought.

'Guess I just made it,' he said weakly. The two girls looked down with shining eyes. Then Alyss had a nice little weep because he looked so badly knocked around.

'Did I do well?' He still didn't know.

'The police think so,' said Alyss. 'And we — we think you're wonderful.'

'We do,' Darling was echoing, and as he lay there, pain burning into him over almost every square inch of his face and body, he was thinking — 'Maybe in six months, maybe twelve . . . '

She held his hand while they put him on a stretcher. He said he could walk, and he probably could have done, but they insisted on carrying him. They always do. She walked by his side while they took him into a room to await an ambulance. And they talked softly, little whispered sentences together. And Alyss kept out of their way, though they would have been surprised if they had realised it.

In the end he got tired of lying down and waiting for an ambulance. His strength was coming back, and he insisted on getting up. Insisted on walking out.

They'd opened up a canteen for the rescue workers. There was a big-gutted, hobo of a man already there. His face was blackened with smoke, but there was no mistaking that figure.

The yawp!

Farran called, 'I might have known. I thought you'd gone under.'

'With a fortune in my pocket? No, sir.' He was being very polite because ladies were present. Not spitting or swearing or anything. Only making a noise as he supped coffee.

Farran said. 'When you've cashed that cheque, you can come around to me for a job.'

The yawp stopped drinking, looked thoughtful. Then he looked wise, 'An' when I get it — '

'I'll fire you like I once promised.'

The yawp came up with his mouth, truculent and fighting as he'd always been. 'The heck, you do that an' I'll bring the whole works out. Me, I'm a labour leader now — '

And then he realised they were all laughing at him.

They shared the same ambulance into town together. Alyss and Darling travelled in with them. Alyss took the big yawp's paw and started to hold it for him. When he looked surprised she said it sort of made things even. And when he looked across at the silent Farran and Darling McMee he understood.

Alyss was thinking, 'It'll be six months, not a year, I'll bet.'

And she was right. It was.

THE END

Other titles in the
Linford Mystery Library:

CALL IN THE FEDS!

Gordon Landsborough

In Freshwater, Captain Lanny was an honest cop with problems: his men and his chief were on the take from the local gangster Boss Myrtle. Bonnie, Myrtle's daughter, was in love with Lanny, but he couldn't pursue the relationship because of her father's criminal activities. Lanny's problems multiplied as Freshwater became threatened by an influx of murderous criminals from New York — a gang of bank raiders, and Pretty Boy, a psychotic murderer of young women. Then Bonnie went missing . . .

THE EDEN MYSTERY

Sydney J. Bounds

Interstellar entrepreneurs, the Eden clan, had opened up new planets, building a galactic empire, governed by the United Worlds' Federation. However, stability is threatened by an impending war between the worlds of Technos and Mogul. The Federation fears intervention by the clan's sole survivor, Kyle Eden. Meanwhile, Hew Keston is investigating the Eden family's history for the media corporation Stereoscopic Inc. But his life is in danger — someone is stopping him from learning the secrets of the Eden clan!

THE LOST FILES OF SHERLOCK HOLMES

Paul D. Gilbert

Dr John Watson finally reopens the lid of his old tin dispatch box and unearths a veritable treasure trove of unpublished tales recounting the remarkable skills of his friend and colleague, Mr Sherlock Holmes. With the detective's consent, we are now finally privileged to witness how Holmes, with his customary brilliance, unravelled the secrets lurking within a too-perfect police constable, a Colonel with a passion for Arthurian mythology, and the public house which never sold a single pint of ale . . .